I0571403

Guiding Light

The Fringes of the Universe
Book One

Cassandra Logan

Guiding Light
The Fringes of the Universe Book One
By Cassandra Logan
Copyright 2016
Cover created by Melody Simmons
ebookindiecovers.com

On the fringes of the universe…

Aimless and with no idea what to do with her life Jutel flies through space just trying to keep her small crew alive.

Kisho, once an Imperial Prince and heir to the Vende throne, has figured out a way to reclaim the fortune denied him.

Thrown together by chance, Jutel isn't sure why she's helping a thief. Kisho just wishes she'd stay in his arms. Separate they're a mess and together they aren't much better, but circumstances throw them on a path neither of them anticipated.

…anything can happen.

Disclaimer- This story has several graphic sex scenes and some mild language.

For my mother

Chapter One

Jutel

Jutel looked into the glass in front of her. It was filled with a vile smelling alien alcohol that she wasn't sure if she liked yet, but beggars couldn't be choosers and she didn't have enough money for something better. Taking a hesitant sip she grimaced, it tasted worse than it smelled, though how that was possible was a miracle of science.

Looking around the bar Jutel took in all the different species. They were mostly humanoid, which wasn't too surprising. Humanoids tended to congregate together, but there were a few other races sprinkled around. It was a typical dive bar, something she was becoming all too familiar with.

What was she doing with her life?

"So how did a little thing like you get a hold of a Nian ship?"

Jutel took another sip of her drink and tried to ignore the alien that had sidled up to her. It never seemed to fail, no matter how disinterested she looked, how aloof, how angry, someone always came up to talk to her. It would be flattering, though still annoying, if they were actually interested, but nine times out of ten they just wanted her ship.

Taking still another sip, the foul liquid was kind of growing on her, Jutel continued to ignore the alien but he just moved closer. Finally, she said, "I'm a Nian."

He made a disgusting noise that sounded like he was trying to laugh and she hoped that he didn't do it again.

"You're black, not blue, you can't be a Nian, everyone knows they've got blue skin."

Gritting her teeth she took another sip to keep herself from responding, in her haste, she swallowed a bit more than she had intended and it burned all the way down.

For some reason, the universe always expected Nians to fit their encyclopedic definition. Nians were supposed to be light blue, friendly, and artists. Jutel was none of the above.

Her skin was blue, though, not the lighter shades most of her people's was, clearly she wasn't the nicest person in the galaxy, though she did like to think she could be nice when the situation called for it, and she was about as artistic as a piece of dirt. She'd chosen the less popular career track on the Nian world, warrior.

Fed up with her evening she shoved away from the bar, leaving the rest of her drink behind. The alien that had been talking to her didn't like being ignored, though, and grabbed her arm.

"I wasn't finished talking to you girlie."

Glancing at his thin spindly fingers she had to restrain herself from breaking them.

"Let me go—please."

See, she could be nice.

He made that horrible noise again then said, "Not likely. I think what I'll do is take you back to that ship of yours. Once I'm done with you, I'll be taking it and everything on board."

He leered and it was an effort not to cringe away from his bad breath. Jutel smiled, it was a smile she'd learned from an Andovian prince, it was part insane, part happy, and part I'm about to fuck you up.

She didn't bother pulling out of his hold, the closer he was the easier the attack would be, instead, she used her free hand to tug on her earlobe and activate her implants. A detailed scan popped up on her retina telling her all she needed to know about the alien species in front of her.

Reaching out she grabbed the front of his shirt and jerked him even closer. As soon as he reached optimum range she slammed her head into his weak chin. He let out a high pitched scream and dropped her arm. Grabbing his shoulders she continued her attack by slamming her knee into his groin, then when his head came down she slammed her knee into his chin one more time.

It was a basic attack, but sometimes those were the best.

The whole thing took less than a minute. She spared the alien howling at her feet only a momentary glance before scanning the room looking for any other possible threats. Men like that rarely worked alone.

Everyone ignored her, drinking their own drinks, and continuing their own conversations. It was just that kind of place.

Leaving the bar she headed back to her ship, The Flower. When they'd landed on the planet they'd only intended to be there for a short time. She almost hadn't left the ship, but being cooped up in space was still new to her even after almost a year. Needing to breathe some unrecycled air she'd left the ship and spent almost an hour sitting in a bar that smelled like vomit. It hadn't been an improvement and she honestly had no idea why she'd done it.

The spaceport they were docked at today wasn't as seedy as they'd been too lately, it was almost respectable. They had several universal chain establishments but they weren't yet big enough for their own police force. Signs around the town showed that wouldn't be the case for much longer. Two men were running for sheriff, and both were promising to clean up the town.

She marched down a road lined with stalls manned by aliens from almost every planet. The closer she got to their docking site the more there were. When people docked on the planet, and most third rate planets for that matter, they tended to set up shop close to their ships. Whether that was because what they were selling was less than legal or because it was a shorter commute, didn't matter. All that mattered was there were too many people for her implants to process all possible threats.

Jutel walked past a group of Tireins clustered around a pile of rusted android parts and rounded the corner to where The Flower was docked. Mal and Bill, her shipmates, were waiting for her, looking up the loading ramp at a tall humanoid alien holding a gun on them.

Walking forward Jutel pulled out her cannon and made sure it was charged before saying, "What the fuck is going on?"

Mal shot her a concerned look, his hands were raised in front of him. Bill just gave her a half smile before saying, "I told you she would get here in time."

Bill was a clairvoyant, he could see bits and pieces of a future that changed frequently, so he wasn't always the most helpful with his advice, but he was a good worker. He wasn't Nian, like Mal and Jutel, he was Olovian. He'd been an Olovian boy when a Nian diplomatic party had freed him from slavery. That was ten years ago and a lot had happened since then. He'd found Mal and Jutel two months ago, asked to join their crew, and they hadn't looked back .

Jutel's focus wasn't on her shipmates, though, it was on the man standing between her and the ship. He was taller than she, which was a bad comparison since she was barely five foot three inches. He wasn't very muscular and looked like he'd missed more meals lately than he'd eaten. He had dark unkempt hair that was plastered to his pale forehead by beads of sweat. His eyes were a crystal clear blue and they held more than a small amount of desperation in them. Knowing that the weapon he was holding on Mal and Bill was a toy made her more worried about what kind of disease he could give them than anything else.

"Stay back! I'm taking this ship. I don't want to hurt you but—"

A disturbance behind them cut him off, glancing quickly over her shoulder Jutel saw the alien she'd just attacked flanked by a group of ten more, coming straight for them.

When she stepped forward the would-be hijacker started to move his weapon to her but in one swift movement, she raised her cannon and fired. The force of the bolt pushed him back up the ramp and knocked him out. Grabbing Mal and Bill she dragged them up the ramp behind him and started yelling out orders. As much as she'd love to stick around and give out some free ass-kicking she had to keep her friends safe.

Bill's Journal

Things are finally starting to happen. Thought I was going to go crazy from boredom. Picked up a new alien that's going to spice things up a bit. Many possible futures ahead.

Mal and Jutel are both depressed, hopefully, this shakes them out of it.

Chapter Two

Kisho

Kisho needed to get off this cesspool of a planet soon or the baron he'd stolen from was going to find him and separate him from his much-needed prize. He'd probably separate his head from the rest of his body while he was at it. It wasn't a pleasant thought, which was why he was looking for a ship.

"I really need to get my own ship it would make these exits so much easier."

Talking to himself was a way to keep his mind focused and off the fact that his stomach was trying to eat itself and doing a bang up job of it. It was not, however, a good way to distract from the little bugs in his hair currently eating up his scalp. He'd been too long on this planet and used up all of his spare and most of his reserve funds.

Clutching the small velvet bag in his pocket he knew it would all be worth it if he could just get off this bloody planet.

Hurrying down the dock, past ship after ship being guarded by either a hulking brute with more muscle than brain cells or a hulking robot that didn't need brain cells, Kisho started to worry. About to settle on the hope that he might be able to talk his way onto a ship being guarded by an idiot he nearly shouted in joy when he spotted a ship that had no guards, just a scrawny kid and a nerdy man standing in front of it.

"Perfect."

Pulling out the toy weapon he'd freed from a stingy toy store owner he tried to put a desperate, crazy glint in his eye, then ran to block the men from the ship.

"Stay back! Your ship is mine now!"

Wow, maybe he should ease back on the drama. The nerd looked at him in shock while the kid looked like he was trying not to laugh. Half the response he was looking for at least. He waved the weapon between the two men, hoping the movement would keep them from noticing that it wasn't a threat.

The nerd, his ears turning pink against his light blue skin, held up his hands and said, "Can we help you with something? I'm sure we don't have to resort to violence. Just let us know what we can do to help, no one has to get hurt."

Nian. The blue skin was a tip off but the unwillingness toward violence was the lock. Kisho had never actually seen one in person, but he'd heard rumors there were a few floating around the universe recently. Interesting.

"Don't worry Mal, he won't hurt us. Jutel will be here soon."

No idea who the teal kid was, though and Kisho didn't like the fact that they were expecting someone else. Maybe this Jutel was their brute force security guard.

"Stay back I'm warning you. I'll just—"

A short curvy woman strode forward a deep frown plastered across her beautiful face. Kisho was blindsided by how attractive she was and immediately decided that if it was the last thing he did he was going to bed her.

"What the fuck is going on?"

The nerd looked concerned but the kid just said, "I told you she would get here in time."

This was Jutel? Definitely not the brute he was concerned about. The lovely creature in front of him was nothing to be afraid of, now he just had to figure out a way to get her on the ship with him.

"Stay back! I'm taking this ship. I don't want to hurt you but—"

The sound of a mob reached his ears and he could see a large group of aliens coming up behind the gorgeous Jutel.

"Shit."

Next thing he knew she aimed a gun at him and everything went dark.

Mal's Notes

Picked up a new alien guest. He looks sickly, but I'm taking care of him. Maybe he'll like Earth Soap Operas, I've just downloaded a whole new series. Excited!

Chapter Three

Jutel

The Flower was a small ship, by Nian standards, but it was exactly what Jutel requisitioned so she had no complaints. One person piloting capabilities, voice controls, the best available Nian security. There were eight personal cabins, a fairly large cargo hold that doubled as a holo suite when it was empty, which was all too often. It had a small galley fully stocked with the latest in Nian tech, and an even smaller cockpit outfitted with the same. Why would anyone need any more than that?

The ship was barely off the line and Jutel was hours away from her first flight when Mal had shown up on her doorstep asking to come along. Mal had been her friend since their first mission to Olovia. He was shy and had an unexplainable attachment to Earth soap operas, but he was wicked smart and loyal to a fault.

"I can't believe you'd even think about going without me. I know what you're going through, I'm going through the same shit too. It makes sense for us to stick together."

At the time, she knew he made sense, but she was still hurting from everything that had happened. Jutel had said something crude and mean and he'd just crossed his arms and waited until she gave in. They hadn't returned to Nian since.

She didn't like to talk about why they left. It was stupid and the fact that she let it bother her so much was humiliating, but what can you do? She tried not to think about it and instead when she remembered home she thought of all the good, her friends and family. She tried not to dwell on all her failures and was currently just trying to keep busy and earn money.

Money, credits, trade, these were completely new concepts for her. Theoretically, she'd know what they were and how they worked but the first time they needed food and didn't have money to buy it had been eye opening. Her goal was to make sure that never happened again.

They took jobs that were probably not what anyone on Nian would be happy with, but they did what they had to. They didn't steal, they didn't kill, and they didn't take advantage. It left them with very few prospects and never any surplus in cash. Their lives right now were about making money to survive and very little else. When Bill joined them he said that was going to change soon. She hoped that was because they'd finally score big and save up a cushion, but she knew she was kidding herself with those hopes.

Now, here they were, two months later escaping an angry mob with a thief passed out in their hold. Things were certainly more exciting, but that wasn't what Jutel had been hoping for.

"What do we do with him?" Mal asked.

"He's going to bring excitement and possibly

become someone very important to all of us."

Rolling her eyes at Bill's vague prediction she tried not to let it get to her. That's just what Bill did, ever since they'd found him on Olovia he'd been making vague predictions. Bill was like an annoying kid brother that you had to love but found yourself putting in a headlock at least once a day. Being around him a lot made you start to feel like you were a part of something bigger. It was frustrating.

"We'll put him in crew quarters, the one furthest from us until he wakes up. Then see where we can drop him."

Picking the alien up with Mal and Bill's assistance, Jutel tried not to notice how light the man was, but there was no help ignoring the smell. Once he was in the open bed Mal ran a medical scanner over him. She told herself they needed to do the check to avoid anything contagious, and that *was* part of it, but her Nian heritage wouldn't allow her not to help someone and if this man needed medical attention the least they could do was offer it.

"He's malnourished, severely dehydrated, and has lice. Other than that, he's fine. I'll get rid of the lice, and I recommend, as a precaution, taking a disinfectant round through the sonic in case it jumped to us when we carried him."

Nodding their heads Bill and Jutel left Mal to it, before separating and heading to their personal quarters. The last thing she needed right now was lice. They'd just dropped off their last batch of cargo and been paid, thankfully, but hadn't had an opportunity to restock. That meant they were low on supplies. Once out of the shower she needed to plot a course to the closest colonized planet so they could resupply.

Her life was so different now. She didn't think about ways to make the universe better she worried about where their next meal would come from. It was humbling and depressing all at the same time.

Standing in the shower stall as the sonic waves washed over her, Jutel tried to plan their next course of action and ignore the depression that was eating away at her. She tried to comfort herself with the fact that they were building a reputation as trusted and efficient couriers. The problem was, they were one ship in a sea of them. So far nothing made them stand out so they just had to rely on first come first serve opportunities and those were almost impossible to plan.

Stepping out of the stall Jutel quickly dressed, pulling on her Nian warrior uniform. She knew she should probably find something else to wear, but she'd spent her entire adult life in that uniform, it was difficult to set it aside. She told Mal it reminded her of where she was from and what their people stood for, it was her little way of not falling completely out of touch with their roots. Most days it helped, others not so much.

She made her way up to the cockpit to search through the navigation computer and noticed they had a message waiting.

"Jutel, this is Zeke, my boys just left a job that I thought you might be interested in. If you're able to get to it first my men say they left behind some premium scrap behind. Load up what you can and I can offer you a fair price."

Relief flooded through her at Zeke's message. She quickly calculated the flight path and was happy to see that there was a planet on the way that they could resupply at. Now she just had to hope no one else got there first.

"Perfect. See, everything's going to work out. We're making friends, creating a name, we'll be good."

She spoke to the empty cockpit as she pulled the planets coordinates.

Zeke was an Andovian that she'd looked up shortly after they left Nian. He owned his own mining operation, but he also still operated a small salvage company on the side. Even better, he'd worked with Nians before and she trusted him, as much as she could trust anyone that is. Whenever he could he sent work their way, but since The Flower wasn't geared for it, there was only so much they could do, which was why they weren't always working.

"Mal, Bill, Zeke sent us a salvage hookup, there's a planet on the way so we'll be able to resupply and drop off the alien."

Jutel spoke over the intercom, plotted the course, and put the ship into hyperdrive.

Watching the darkness outside calmed her nerves and the feeling of doom in her stomach, which was good because they'd both been getting worse the longer she was out here. Maybe it was time to head home?

"What are you thinking about?" Bill snuck up behind her, but she was used to it at this point and didn't tackle him to the ground.

Sometimes it was difficult to take him seriously. Bill was barely nineteen, still a child by Nian standards, but he'd been through a lot in his short life, even if his baby face hid it well. He was the de facto leader of the Olovian's on Nian and by all accounts did a stellar job, though he spent a majority of his time out in space lately. His people had been through more than anyone ever should, many of them still suffered, but Bill made sure they were all taken care of.

Hesitating Jutel almost didn't say anything, but it wasn't her way to bottle things up and that's exactly what she'd been doing. Maybe talking about it would help because so far each day was becoming worse than the last. She felt—hopeless. Nothing she did seemed to matter, to her, to her crew, to the universe outside. This wasn't what she thought her life would be.

"I was wondering if we should head home. I don't know why we're even out here anymore Bill. Why did we *ever* come out here? I know why you're here, you like to wander, you're rarely on the planet long these days, but why are Mal and I here? I don't like running cargo or picking up salvage, I'm not making the world or universe a better place. What's my purpose, Bill?"

"Do you need a purpose?"

His eyes bored into hers and she wondered what he saw. Looking down at her hands resting in her lap Jutel said, "Yes, I do. I didn't think I did, but if the last year has taught me anything, it's that I need direction. I need to be working toward something that's more than just making sure we have food, but how can I when that goal takes up so much of my time?"

She didn't' cry, Jutel never cried, but she desperately wished for some kind of release from the overwhelming sense of apathy that she was feeling. It was worse than anger and it just seemed to suck her down further and further.

Bill placed his hand on her shoulder and squeezed. "If you're really seeking a change then I can assure you, you're about to get it."

He didn't say anything else before leaving her alone in the cockpit. She returned to her starring contest with the cosmos and wondered what Bill had seen.

Bill's Journal

Jutel says she needs a purpose, that's narrowed the futures I'm seeing down. I'm worried about her, though, she needs more than a purpose. She needs to find what makes her happy.

New guy is hilarious. Mal finally has someone else to share his stories with, relieved.

Chapter Four

Kisho

When Kisho woke up he was surprised to see the nerd standing over him with what appeared to be a medical scanner. A quick assessment of his body told him that the lice were gone and despite his sudden flight from whatever it was that shot him, he felt fine. If he was being honest with himself, and he prided himself on being honest with at least himself, he could admit that he hadn't felt this good in a long time.

Once that was out of the way he said, "What am I doing here? What's going on? Do you have any idea who I am?"

Intimidation didn't always work, but it was an old habit that he found himself relying on. It was also difficult to pull off when you're lying prone on a bed with no recollection as to how you got there. Still, Kisho pulled it off admirably and the nerd's ears started to turn red.

"You're on The Flower, you're going to be fine, we won't hurt you. My name's Mal, I just completed a medical scan and was able to get rid of your lice. I've got some rations right here and some water. Try and eat slow you're malnourished and you could get sick."

Maybe he hadn't been as intimidating as he thought. The nerd, Mal, hadn't said anything about how he'd gotten there, though, it was fairly obvious. Jutel, the beautiful woman that had momentarily distracted him from his plan to steal her ship had shot him and they'd dragged him to this cabin. As much as he'd wanted to bed her before, he wasn't so sure anymore.

Kisho was a rogue, he could certainly dish out as well as he could take, but some things were just unattractive, and being shot by a gorgeous woman was one of them. Oh well, she had no idea what she was missing.

Slowly eating the tasteless rations provided to him Kisho began pumping Mal for information. When he was told they were no longer on the planet he started to relax further. He'd already checked his pocket and the reason for his need to get off the planet in a hurry was still there. Honestly, these people had done him a huge favor so in return he'd already decided not to steal from them.

Well—unless they had something really amazing.

The ship was pretty amazing.

No, he wouldn't do that to them.

Probably.

He'd see.

Maybe.

It was really nice and he'd just seen his cabin. The bed was comfortable, the lighting excellent, and it didn't look like a clunky freighter, it was clean. Though a bit bare for his taste. Weren't Nians supposed to be artists?

His mind whirled with these thoughts as he wolfed down the food he'd been given. It was like eating cardboard, definitely below his normal fare, but since he hadn't had his normal fare in over a year it was adequate.

When he was done eating Mal used the communicator to contact Jutel, letting her know he was fine being taken from the planet. Apparently Kisho hadn't done as good a job as he thought hiding his joy. He was going to have to work on doing a better job hiding his emotions, his father would have greatly disapproved of how easily he was being read. Of course, his father had never gone so long without food. Then again his father had also been murdered.

Chatting with Mal he was caught off guard when Jutel walked through his door. She was just as beautiful as he remembered and that immediately made him angry. He couldn't sleep with her, she had shot him, but she was physical perfection. Life could be so cruel.

"You shot me!"

Her expression didn't change and he couldn't help but admire her for it. "You were pointing a gun at my friends, albeit a toy, and trying to steal my ship. I regret nothing."

Good, someone in authority should never apologize. She just kept on racking up points in his favor. He decided to test her further. "I could have been seriously injured. I demand compensation for the distress you've caused me."

Her simple one-word answer was almost enough to add her back to the list of women he had to make love to. She was truly spectacular, standing before him, arms crossed, a look of absolute boredom on her face. It was time to let her know exactly who he was and put her back in her place.

"That's it? No? Are you kidding me? I am the Imperial Crown Prince Kisho of Vende and I demand retribution!"

He ended up adding more drama than he had intended, but surely she would get the idea. Even a Nian should know of the Imperial family, they were famous across the galaxy for their wealth and power. Instead of the awe he expected to receive, though, she ignored his title completely. In fact, she told him they were going to drop him off on the planet Benjo of all places. Benjo! Who in their right mind went there?

His brain processed the possibilities and he quickly landed on a better option, glancing up he realized that Jutel was leaving.

"I have a favor to ask."

Better to word it that way, so that they would feel less inclined to say no. His favor was small, wouldn't cost them more than what they were already doing, and so saying yes to him would cost them nothing and make them feel good. Hopefully, they wouldn't look further than the surface of his request.

"I have some business on the planet Ostara, it's in the same system as Benjo so it won't add any time to your trip. I request that you drop me off there. That's all I'm asking after you kidnapped me, I think it's more than reasonable."

Reminding them of the kidnapping was just a less than subtle way of guiding them in his direction. Jutel's frown was enough to stir Kisho's cock beneath the sheets, thank all that is holy for his pants or things could have been embarrassing. She was definitely going back under the do column, right under that weather girl on that one planet. What was that's planet name? Never mind, it didn't matter.

She agreed, of course, and then left him alone. Mal left shortly after which gave Kisho an opportunity to clean up. There was a laundry device built into the wall so he stripped off his clothes, hid his treasure, and jumped in the sonic shower. Stepping out he felt cleaner than he had in ages.

He missed being on top of the universe. So much had gone so wrong in such a short amount of time that he hadn't had much time to think about it. His mood grew dark and Kisho's mind swirled with murky thoughts until he pulled his clean clothes on. Looking around his cabin he decided the best course of action was to explore the ship. He had two days to figure out if stealing it would be worthwhile or too much of a hassle. A Nian ship would make a lovely statement.

Mal's Notes

I will never understand why my people have not embraced soap operas. They are a fountain of creativity and drama surpassed by nothing made on Nian. I feel a renewed sense of purpose to pick up writing my own. I've messaged Lucy and Angela and they've given me amazing advice. I feel like this is what I've been searching for, this will help me overcome my bad mood. I will pour all of my negative emotions, my doubt, and fear, into these stories and will come out on the other side a new man.

Chapter Five

Jutel

"Jutel our guest is awake if you'd like to question him." Mal's voice interrupted Jutel's contemplation an hour after Bill left her.

"How is he?"

"Better now that I told him we're no longer on the planet."

A sense of foreboding started to creep it's way up her spine as she made her way to the alien thief, it wasn't just Bill's warning, her gut was telling her something important was about to happen.

It only took a minute to arrive at the alien's quarters and the door was already open. Stepping through she found the thief sitting up in bed with a surprisingly charming smile on his face as he spoke to Mal who looked more than a little bit flattered by whatever was being said. The charming smile disappeared, though, when he caught sight of her.

"You shot me."

His gaze was accusing but she just raised an eyebrow at him and said, "You were pointing a gun at my friends, albeit a toy, and trying to steal my ship. I regret nothing."

"I could have been seriously injured. I demand compensation for the distress you've caused me."

She crossed her arms and met his stare before saying, "No."

"That's it? No? Are you kidding me? I am the Imperial Crown Prince Kisho of Vende and I demand retribution!"

This bedraggled man in front of them was a prince? Maybe a prince of a long dead kingdom, but certainly not Vende and it's immense fortune. This meeting was not going like she thought it would. After Bill's remarks, she assumed something—different, less annoying and more lucrative.

Ignoring his title Jutel said, "We're on our way to the planet Benjo, we'll drop you off there, it should take about two standard days to arrive. If Mal hasn't told you already we've cleared up your lice and we will provide you with a week's worth of rations to help you once on the planet. Until then, stay out of my way."

"I have a favor to ask." His voice was pompous and condescending, as though he were about to reward her with what he was about to say, even though she didn't deserve it.

Jutel glanced at Mal but all he did was shrug his shoulders and shake his head. Growing quickly more annoyed by the man but unable to stop herself she asked, "What?"

"I have some business on the planet Ostara, it's in the same system as Benjo so it won't add any time to your trip, I request that you drop me off there. That's all I'm asking after you kidnapped me, I think it's more than reasonable."

She frowned at him and walked to the computer panel on the wall by the door. Pulling up Ostara a quick search showed that he was right, it wouldn't add any more time to their trip so they should still get to the junk debris before anyone else. It was a reasonable request and once again not what she expected from this man.

"Fine, I'll make the changes. We'll drop you off on the planet and part ways there."

This time, he didn't stop her when she left.

Two days passed quickly, with Jutel spending most of it in the cockpit avoiding their guest. Kisho spent a lot of time roaming the ship but he didn't steal anything, Jutel made sure of that, so she saw no need in hindering his exploration.

Mal thought he was interesting, and spent the entire time reading up on Kisho's lineage, then quizzing him on everything from popular cuisine to common hand gestures. In return, Kisho asked him a never ending supply of questions on the soap operas Mal watched in his spare time. It was an odd relationship, but at least, they were keeping each other entertained.

"Did you know that his family has led the Vende planet for over a thousand years? They were instrumental in getting the planet accepted into the United Universal Aid Coalition and are in fact one of its founding planets."

"No, of course, I didn't know that, why would I care?"

Mal's ears turned pink and she felt a little bad for snapping at him, but she couldn't help it. Bringing up the UUAC was like rubbing salt into an open wound. She'd wanted Nian to be able to rejoin the coalition, had made it her life's goal, only to be very handily shut down by them. Of course, that was after she'd jumped through their hundreds of hoops and done more than a few things she wasn't proud of. Mal knew all of that, though, and should have never brought it up to her.

Clearing his throat Mal said, "Changing the subject, what are our plans after the salvage mission?"

Frustrated Jutel bit her tongue to keep from making another sharp comment. It wasn't his fault that she didn't know what they were going to do. It wasn't anyone's fault, but it didn't keep her from wanting to beat something. Quickly standing up she ignored his question and said, "I'm going to exercise. Comm me if something happens."

She left the bridge and could have sworn she heard Mal let out a deep breath. She'd had a short fuse these last few days and she knew she'd taken his head off more than once, but if it bothered his so damn much why didn't he step up and take the lead? Why was she the one that always had to make decisions?

Cueing up a strenuous program, the holo suite materialized around her, displaying an involved obstacle course that should slake her thirst for destruction. It wasn't one of the more violent programs available, she shied away from those, Jutel didn't like how they made her feel. As though—she'd lost control and become a mindless killing machine. It wasn't pleasant, but her emotions or lack thereof, had her gravitating toward those programs more and more.

Three hours later, lathered in sweat, the program shut down. Breathing deep, her chest heaving from the workout she'd just put herself through, she almost missed Kisho watching her. Almost.

"What are you doing?"

"Watching you."

Frowning she asked, "Why?"

A charming smile came across his lips and he said, "Do I need a reason to watch a beautiful woman?"

She didn't like the fact that his words made her feel tingly. Her frown deepened and she focused on the fact that statistics told her that all he was after was her ship. Walking past him she ignored his smile and the way it made her feel and made her way to her room to clean up.

She wanted a lot of things right now, but a relationship was not one of them. She had half an hour before they landed on Ostara, plenty of time to get ready. Once there she wouldn't have to see Kisho or his crystal blue eyes ever again.

He wasn't even that attractive, he still needed to gain a good fifteen pounds before he lost the look of a skeleton. Plus he was so pompous and full of himself, and he was a thief. A Nian would never get into a relationship with a thief. It was not done.

Still, he thought she was beautiful.

Groaning, Jutel rested her forehead on the wall of the shower stall and did her best to ignore the waves as they cascaded over her body, touching her with the softness of a lover's hands.

A minute later she stepped out and was more frustrated than ever. Now, not only did she have no idea what to do with her life and the lives of her crew, she needed to take care of a libido that had no business acting up.

"I'm going to buy a sexbot, that way I'll never be in this position again." She shook her head at the statement and added, "Stupid woman, sexbots cost money, and you can barely afford to feed yourself."

Gritting her teeth she decided she'd just have to take care of it the old fashioned way, but that would have to wait until they'd dealt with the resupply. It would take twelve hours to get to the junk, that was more than enough time to deal with her issue.

Bill's Journal

I've never met a Nian or Olovian as stubborn as Jutel. She's resisting her attraction to Kisho like he has the plague. Of course, if I hadn't seen his clean medical scan for myself I could have easily believed he did.

Mal is writing a soap opera, hopefully, that will get him to shut up about them. Probably not.

The future is…fuzzy. I see a few possibilities but something seems odd.

I'm having fun messing with Kisho, I will miss him if the future we end up in doesn't include him.

Chapter Six

Kisho

Ostara was exactly as he remembered it. They landed in the city of his choice and he walked off the ramp enjoying the fresh air the ocean breeze sent his way. Ostara was more than eighty percent oceans which made it a paradise planet. Things were naturally a bit more expensive here, but the tradeoff was completely acceptable. Just look at the views.

This was exactly what he needed. The climate was controlled by an amazing feat of technology and every day on Ostara was another day in the heaven of your choice.

Quickly leaving Mal, Jutel, and the rather creepy Bill behind Kisho decided to spare them the sorrow of stealing their ship and instead hoped to never see them again. Mal was exactly what he'd thought he was on his first inspection, a nerd. The man had quizzed him on history and policies for most of their two-day trip and if he ever had to explain societal norms to someone he'd probably shoot himself. Of course, the stories he'd watched with the man had been riveting, though, Kisho would never say it out loud.

Jutel would be missed but being honest with himself he knew that he'd get over her. Especially since he had the women of Ostara to help him along. Jutel could have been an excellent distraction, but it wasn't meant to be and he was more than willing to let her go.

When he'd left them, taking the rations they offered, of course, Bill had just smiled and said that they would see him again. The boy was weird, like super weird, like scary weird. He was always making vague predictions about the future like he somehow knew what was going to happen. The only known psychic race was the Velusions and they had large heads, huge eyes, and didn't leave their planet. It was kind of admirable that Jutel and Mal took care of someone like Bill who was clearly a few rubies short of a full crown, but only admirable from a distance.

Walking through the happy crowds of people Kisho searched for a specific store. It was the only place he trusted to perfectly judge the quality of the loot he was carrying. He finally rounded a corner and saw exactly what he was looking for, a Tiger Inc. Electronics Store.

He was grinning as he walked through the door and easily sidestepped the greeter that gave him the stink eye. He was a prince they couldn't keep him out, even if he was poorly dressed.

Making a beeline straight for a console with the most state of the art technology available Kisho pulled out the velvet bag holding his prize. Reaching into the depths he pulled out a small bio-reader, he put it on the appropriate port of the console, applied his thumb, and waited.

It took longer than he expected and by the time

a readout appeared he'd started to sweat. Finally, the words he'd been waiting to see appeared: YOU ARE A DIRECT DESCENDANT OF EMPEROR ALPHA DAWN OF VENDE

In the middle of the Tiger Inc. store, he let out a shout, dancing around until he noticed security heading his way. Taking the bio-reader from the console he left before they could embarrass themselves by trying to throw him out. Really, you'd think the people in an establishment as renowned as Tiger Inc. would know royalty when they saw it.

A weight like a stone left his shoulders and there was a bounce in his step as he made his way down the street. He'd worked over a year to get this bio-reader, countless hours planning, his entire paltry fortune spent, to obtain this small bit of tech. The only known device, outside of the royal archives, that had the original Vende Emperor's DNA. There was more data on the bio-reader, congenital stuff, gene stuff, but none of that mattered to Kisho, all that mattered was he finally had proof that his two-timing bastard of a cousin twice removed by marriage had no true claim to the throne.

"Just wait until I get home. He'll be begging me to disappear, he'll pay anything I want."

Giggling uncontrollably Kisho almost missed the man falling into step behind him. He was about to shake it off as a coincidence when someone started matching his pace ahead, and he knew he was being boxed in. His eyes darted around trying to find an escape.

He'd been stupid, he'd let himself get distracted from the fact that his cousin had spies everywhere. They must have been tipped off when he'd used the bio-reader, but how had they gotten here so fast?

Seeing an opening he darted out of the line of people on the sidewalk and through the moving vehicles on the street. He was never in any real danger, all the cars on Ostara were driven by autopilot, but it was still impressive to see and he heard several women scream in terror.

That's right ladies, Imperial Prince Kisho risks life and limb as he brilliantly out maneuvers his thieving cousin's henchmen. Don't worry, though, there's plenty to go around.

The mental commentary caused him to miss the one car that wasn't stopping. It was a small sports model, top of the line, only twenty ever made, and it plowed right into him. Thankfully it wasn't going at its top speed or he would have been splattered on the pavement, instead, it was likely he was going to need knee replacements in his forties.

"Stupid rich mother fu—"

Seeing the suits beginning to close in on him, Kisho stood up, stumbled, then sprinted down the road toward the oncoming traffic. Yeah, yeah, he'd already been hit once, but he was paying better attention this time. Dodging through the stopping cars he was able to put a small lead between him and his pursuers before they joined him on the much less crowded roadway.

A flash of deep navy out of the corner of his eye reminded him that there was a ship docked, very close, that he happened to know everything about. Smiling he made a sharp turn, then another, then another, until he was on the docking platform where the Flower was located.

The ramp was down, no one was outside, everything was working out in his favor. He was halfway to the bridge when he felt the ship move.

"Shit."

Either someone else had decided to steal this baby or he'd missed the fact that the crew was on board. Hadn't they needed to stop for supplies? There was no way someone could resupply in the short time he'd been gone.

"Damnit."

Well, there was nothing else he could do, they were leaving and he needed to get off the planet fast. Sighing he made his way to his cabin and plotted the best way to let them know he was back. Settling into his cot he smiled, they'd be happy to see him. After all, he was the Vende Imperial Prince and he was about to come into a very large fortune. Everyone loved being around rich people.

Mal's Notes

Well for about five minutes I saw paradise. There was a beach just yards away from our dock that had the whitest sand I've ever seen. I could easily picture a beautiful, blond, bombshell walking down it wearing a white dress that was plastered to her curvy body by the breeze.

The story I'm writing is boring, trying to think up ways to spice it up. I've thrown out what I've written at least ten times so far. You'd think with all that I've watched I would be able to pump this thing out. Oh well. Hopefully, I get some inspiration sometime soon.

Maybe I'll use my blond bombshell in my story. We'll see…

Chapter Seven

Jutel

"Who in their right mind recommends that planet for resupply? What about our ship screams money? We're living on space rations for crying out loud!"

Jutel ranted in the cockpit after Mal and Bill left her alone. The minute they'd landed they'd been hit with a docking fee that had taken half their money. Then when they arrived at the first establishment promising food they'd nearly fallen over at the prices. Fifty UUAC credits for an eighth of a space ration. Most planets charged fifty UUAC credits for a crate of five hundred rations. It was ludicrous!

"I can't believe—we've wasted so much—if I ever see that stupid Prince Kisho whatever his name is I'm going to ring his neck!"

She was so angry she couldn't finish her sentences and violence seemed like a perfectly acceptable response. Never in her entire life had someone made her so angry, and she'd dealt with slavers and bureaucrats.

Fuming she entered the coordinates to the planet Benjo, which was where she'd wanted to go in the first place. It would only take a few minutes, but they'd have to pay another docking fee though she'd already confirmed this was a small fraction of the Ostara's. Then they had to hope that food wasn't as expensive because they couldn't afford another delay.

Her fingers slammed across the console, she jerked at the flight stick, and The Flower made its hardest landing ever. The ship shook, briefly from the contact, but Jutel was too mad to care. Making sure her cannon was still strapped to her side she stomped from the cockpit and toward the exit ramp, where Mal and Bill were supposed to be waiting for her.

Jutel rounded the corner from the cockpit and came face to face with an angry and agitated Kisho. "What the hell are you doing? We're still in the god damn system, you can't stop now! We have to—"

There was no hesitation when she grabbed her cannon and fired. He didn't have far to fly this time since they were in a corridor of the ship, but she didn't even flinch when he made a sickly thud against the wall. She knew he was still alive, she hadn't given him a full force shot, but he was going to have a nasty bump on his head.

Mal and Bill came running at the sound and she grinned at them. "Suddenly I feel so much better. Let's get the supplies taken care of and we'll head to the coordinates Zeke gave us."

Mal's eyes were wide in shock but Bill just shared her grin.

Swallowing Mal said, "I think I'll stay here with Imperial Prince Kisho and make sure he's okay."

"Suit yourself. Bill are you still coming?"

"I wouldn't miss it."

His grin grew and if Jutel had been paying

better attention, instead of replaying the moment Kisho flew through the air over and over in her mind, she might have worried at Bill's level of enthusiasm. Instead, she left the ship in a much-improved mood and went in search of a resupply location.

The change on the planets wasn't as huge as she'd expected from the difference in docking fees. In fact, the few things she'd noticed on Ostara, the salty breeze, and beautiful view, were the same on Benjo. There was a marked difference, though, in the number of people. Ostara had been crowded, filled to the brim with aliens, but Benjo was almost overwhelmingly native species. It was—interesting.

They walked about a mile before they came to a store that advertised space rations. Entering Jutel braced herself for the price and was once again pleasantly surprised to see a number much more to her liking. Chatting with the store owner she discovered the two planets had an interesting cycle. For a while, one would be a tourist trap for the wealthy and elite while the natives commuted from the other planet. That continued until someone 'discovered' the other planet and how empty it was and the tourists would migrate over, the natives would just switch home worlds.

Jutel kept waiting for Bill to jump in on the conversation, he usually loved to chime in with his little insights into the future, but his nose was wrinkled and he was studying the front of the store as though any minute he expected something to happen. Growing increasingly uneasy she paid for a crate, added as many fresh items as she could afford, and paid for transport.

They had fifteen minutes before everything would be delivered to The Flower and even with Bill's worrisome attitude, Jutel wasn't ready to head back to the ship. With directions from the store owner for the best view in town, she started walking toward the seaside cliffs. Bill stayed behind.

Taking deep breaths of the glorious fresh air Jutel did her best not to think about everything that was going on in her life. She tried to block out the hopelessness and depression and just think about the view in front of her. The water crashed against the cliffs, but she was too high up to feel the spray. Looking down she watched as wave after wave disappeared against the unmoving rocks.

She forced herself to look up and at the vast ocean in front of her. Birds flew high in the air, occasionally screaming out at each other. She could see a few people sunning themselves on the beach to the north of the cliffs and the laughter of children floated up to her ears.

Tearing her eyes away from the sight she thrust her hands into her pockets and frowned at the view. It was beautiful, the whole place was like a picture from a storybook, and she hadn't been anywhere this nice and calming in a year, but it just made everything worse.

She could find sights like this and more back home. Why was she here? What was she doing with her life? She should be home on Nian, paired up and on her second child. Instead, she was flying aimlessly through space trying not to starve to death. Why had she let one failure, albeit a massive one, deter her course? Would Ambassador Talina, her role model, and idol have given up? No. Well—at the very least she would have given herself another goal to work toward. Why hadn't Jutel done that?

"I'm tired."

The words slipped from her mouth and she

realized just how true they were. She and Mal had been so energized after their first mission that they hadn't paused once in their pursuit to have Nian rejoin the ranks of the United Universe Aid Coalition. Mal had filled her head with the romance of the place, how they worked to bring aid and hope to even the most desperate backwater planet and she'd loved the idea. She didn't want to be another Nian female destined to pop out five babies while her career was put on hold. She was a warrior and she'd found her cause, with Mal by her side they couldn't fail.

Only they had.

Mal wasn't a leader, which wasn't his fault. He was smart but that wasn't enough. Jutel had convinced herself that she could do that part. Except, Jutel wasn't a leader either, at least not a diplomatic one, and that's what the UUAC had required. She'd bungled one thing after another until she'd pissed off half the members of the UUAC, it hadn't come as any surprise when her request had been rejected. It hadn't helped when the Nian council had told her they wouldn't have accepted even if she'd secured a place.

"Jutel we have more problems than we can comfortably handle as is, without adding the galaxies."

That had just infuriated her more. Her planet had been great, once. They'd been leaders in the galaxy, the best artists in the universe, with technology generations ahead of the others. Now they were isolated and barely managing to maintain their population, even with strict population laws.

Shaking her head Jutel tugged her ear to activate her implants and check the time. Twenty minutes had passed.

"Crap."

Turning around she mentally berated herself for wasting five minutes thinking about things she couldn't change. She had to get back to The Flower and take off. They had to get to the space debris, as it was they were probably too late.

Jogging through the town, her implant still running, Jutel paid only half a mind to the information streaming across her retina. It was second nature to her and she barely registered she was doing it until something caught her attention. Slowing her pace she called the data back up and discovered that someone was following her.

Stopping in the middle of the empty sidewalk she waited to see what the two men her implants had detected had planned for her. To her knowledge, she hadn't done anything wrong and there should be no reason for someone to attack her, but her limited experience in the universe had taught her that didn't matter. They could want her ship, not going to happen, they could want her body, seriously not going to happen.

She didn't have to wait long to find out. The one moving up behind her grabbed both of her arms, holding her in place. There were several things she could have done to break his hold, but she still had no idea what they wanted so she decided the wait.

The man in front of her continued walking until he was only a foot in front of her, his face had no distinguishing features and seemed wrong in some way. Her display identified his origin as Venedian, which begged the question, what had Kisho done.

"Excuse me, but I would really appreciate it if you'd let me go. I haven't done anything and I really don't like being touched without permission." She tried to sound friendly and unthreatening but that was never her strong suit.

"You will not speak unless we ask you a direct question. We represent His Majesty the Reigning Emperor of Vende. Why did you leave Ostara and come to Benjo? Are you hiding the thief and impersonator Kisho?"

Well, that answered that question. Frowning at the man in front of her, the man that hadn't identified himself, her brain processed all of her possible responses. The truth was always a favorite. It was easy to remember and didn't often get you in trouble later on. A lie, though, might be the best response in this situation. She didn't know why these men were looking for Kisho, and clearly it wasn't to hand out an award. About to probe for more before giving her answer, she felt something prick her skin on the back of her neck.

Jerking forward, but not out of her captor's grasp, she said, "What are you doing to me? I haven't done anything!"

"We aren't going to hurt you, we just want to make sure you tell us the truth."

The man's face was expressionless like he was an android programmed without a personality, he stood there waiting for the drugs to kick in. Jutel could feel a coolness spreading through her body and an alert popped up on her retina display. Her nanites were already springing into action, swarming whatever had been injected into her body and destroying it. They didn't know that, though, so she tried to put a complacent look on her face. Whatever she was doing seemed to be right, because the man holding her loosened his grip.

"Now, answer the question, where is the

fugitive Kisho? We know he was seen getting off your ship, and you left Ostara shortly after we lost him. Was he on board with you?"

She tried to slur her words when she spoke, "No, he wasn't. He conned us into taking him to Ostara, but when we docked he disappeared. We needed food, but it was too expensive there, so we came to Benjo. I didn't see him on Ostara after he left us."

Keeping it short and sweet seemed like her best option and she tried to keep it as close to the truth as possible. Technically, it hadn't been until they'd landed on Benjo that she'd seen Kisho.

Why she felt the need to twist the truth for Kisho, she wasn't sure, but selling him out to these men seemed wrong. He was an ass and incredibly annoying, but he hadn't done anything to her or her friends that called for a response that harsh. It went against her Nian training, but she'd done more than a few things that did that, this was just the latest.

He studied her face before looking at his partner over her shoulder and nodding his head. The second man let her go and she pretended to stumble.

"We will scan your ship and confirm that you aren't lying. If you are found hiding the fugitive you will be prosecuted to the full extent of the law."

They began marching her back to The Flower.

That could have gone better, but things still weren't too bad, as long as she could contact her crew she could keep everyone safe. Her nanites had counteracted the truth drug they'd given her, she'd already received a notification that her system had been cleaned, but these men weren't completely stupid so she couldn't just do a ship decontamination sweep. That would erase all evidence of Kisho being onboard and they already knew he had been. That meant she had only one option and she had to get ahold of Mal and Kisho had to cooperate.

The range on her implants wasn't far, and she didn't know the codes or have the time to hack them to gain Benjo's wireless network, so it wasn't until she reached The Flower's range that she was able to send her warning to Mal. Crossing her fingers she hoped he got it in time.

The two men said nothing and they only passed a couple people on their way back to the ship, none of them seemed eager to jump to Jutel's rescue. She didn't blame them, she was a stranger and the men seemed official. It was alright, though, Jutel knew that once she got them on her home ground they didn't stand a chance. Nians didn't like violence and they didn't believe in taking a sentient beings life, but that in no way meant they couldn't defend themselves. Plus, Jutel wasn't the best of Nians anyway.

They reached the ship without once seeing Bill and Jutel hoped that he was already on board. She didn't know how this was going to go down exactly and she didn't want to have to wait around for him. Bill was smart, he could see the freaking future, surely he was on the ship.

Marching up the lowered gangplank she waited for any kind of orders or indication of what she needed to do but it wasn't until they were in the cargo hold that they spoke to her again.

"Stay here while we run our search. Your ship is small, it won't take long."

They separated and left her alone. As soon as they were out of her sight she walked to the computer screen by the door and pulled up the security feed. She located Mal in his room reading a book, but didn't see Kisho or Bill. She was relieved about the first and concerned about the second.

The Venedians systematically swept through the ship, she saw no form of scanner and they didn't touch anything as they moved. When they came to Mal's room he feigned surprise, poorly, but they didn't do anything to him except ask the same questions they'd asked Jutel. He lied, poorly, but they didn't do anything else to him.

The whole sweep took less than an hour and when they started heading back to the cargo bay she shut down the computer screen and moved back to the center of the bay.

"We have found proof that the traitor was on your ship, but we were not able to find any proof that he remained. You are free to go."

That was it. They made their declaration then left. Breathing a sigh of relief she performed a scan of the ship to make sure they hadn't left anything behind. While that was running she paced, waiting for Bill to turn up. They needed to get into the air before Kisho did something else stupid and brought an army down on them. The computer dinged at the completion of the scan and Bill walked in at the same time.

The problem, now, was that Bill wasn't alone. He was towing behind him a young woman holding a small bundle. Uneasy, Jutel eyed the bundle, then turned her gaze to Bill. "Where have you been? We need to leave, Kisho has got Venedians searching for him. They've already searched the ship, but we need to leave before they decide to come back."

"This is Dido, I told her we could help her and

her baby."

Just then the small bundle let out an ear splitting scream and Dido clumsily tried to shush it. Rubbing her head where a headache was blossoming Jutel tried to figure out why the universe hated her so much.

Bill's Journal

While picking up supplies with Jutel my ability to see the future went completely dark. The last thing I saw was a beautiful Venedian woman holding a baby and I found her hiding behind the store by a crate. Naturally my only course of action was to bring her with us.

Chapter Eight

Kisho

The cramped locker Kisho was in provided almost no light or even room to move. It was like a coffin and the longer he stayed in it the smaller the space seemed. It figured, just when he got what he needed to finally gain the fortune owed to him, he got shoved into a small compartment where he was clearly going to suffocate. Sure Mal was just trying to help, but if he'd really wanted to help they could have left the planet. Jutel and Bill would have been fine, the Venedians weren't after them.

It felt like days had passed when Mal finally opened the hidden locker. The light was welcoming and Kisho stumbled out taking deep breaths, trying to fill his empty lungs.

"Are you okay?"

"No, I'm not okay! I nearly died in there! I'm going to file a complaint, those lockers are not fit to store a sack of potatoes let alone a living breathing man."

Mal stood there as Kisho vented his frustrations

for a solid ten minutes. When he finally calmed down Mal offered him some water and strongly suggested the use of a shower stall.

Fuming at the implication that he smelled Kisho took a sip of his water and prepared to put Mal firmly back into place. Seriously, how dare the man make such a rude suggestion, before he could begin, though, a loud shrieking cry cut him off.

Wincing Mal looked over his shoulder toward an open cabin door. They had hidden Kisho in a storage locker concealed behind a panel in the hallway of the crew's quarters and the open door was on the other end of the long hallway. From that distance, nothing should be that loud.

Kisho frowned and tossed his empty water at Mal before striding down the hallway to investigate.

"What in blazes is making that horrible noise?"

A harried young woman looked up at him. She was young and sweet looking, so not his type at all, but it was the baby in her arms that was making the noise. She cringed away from Kisho. Bill stood in the corner looking unsure and confused, which was a new look for him.

The child didn't care that its screams were echoing through the room or that its mother was clearly terrified. It didn't even care that it was giving Kisho a splitting headache, which was really inconsiderate of it.

Reaching out Kisho snatched the child from the mother's loose grasp. He plopped the child, which turned out to be a girl, on the bed and swiftly bundled it up tight. With that done he picked her up and began rocking and humming an old Venedian lullaby.

When the child finally settled down and the song ended Kisho said, "I see we picked up some new passengers. I want to make it clear that since I've been here longest I have dibs on getting to pitch fits. I don't take kindly to people who try and usurp my power, so keep that in mind little chick."

The baby girl didn't make a sound because she had fallen asleep. The mother stood up and transferred the soothed infant from his arms back to hers. Bill looked—stunned, which put a smug look on Kisho's face. He was a man of many talents.

"How did you do that?"

Jutel's voice came from behind him and he turned to see her studying him. He grinned and said, "Children love me. They recognize authority and know that I'm powerful."

She snorted and said, "More likely they recognize a kindred spirit."

Kisho didn't respond, his powers were clearly lost on Jutel, which just made her all that appealing. Since he was going to be staying on The Flower, surely he'd have an opportunity to bed its captain. He took a step toward her, his most charming smile across his lips, but as he drew closer she curled her nose at him.

"Take a shower, please, you reek of body odor."

Glaring at her Kisho prepared to tell her exactly what he thought of her lack of manners but she turned around and left. That infernal woman, she had no respect for his position and power. He was an emperor!

Unofficially.

Still, he was one, until he could convince his cousin to pay him lots and lots of money, then he wouldn't care about titles.

He glanced at the others in the room, all of whom were avoiding meeting his gaze before he followed Jutel's exit and made his way to his room. Fine since everyone seemed to think he smelled, he'd take a shower. It's not like he didn't enjoy using the sonic, it was almost as good as having a woman rub her hands all over him. Almost.

As the waves washed over his naked body Kisho closed his eyes to imagine the woman of his dreams. Instead of the usual buxom red head that loved telling him how magnificent he was, how large and intimidating, but oh so worth the momentary discomfort. When he closed his eyes Jutel was there, frowning at him in disappointment.

His eyes flew open and he slammed the shower off. "Curse that woman. Can't even take a shower without her interfering. I should have stolen the ship and left them on Ostara."

That would have been a kindness compared to what she was doing to him. In fact, the soonest he could he was going to take the ship and leave them all behind. That would serve her right.

Mal's Notes

Wow, Bill brought a woman and a baby on board. Jutel doesn't seem too happy about it, but we needed to get off Benjo quick so she didn't argue. She didn't even argue about keeping Kisho on board. What's up with those two anyway?

Dido seems—odd. She doesn't seem to know what to do with her daughter. I'd almost think it wasn't hers if the little sprite didn't look exactly like her. They're Venedian, which is interesting. I had no idea they were such a well-traveled race?

All this drama has done wonders for my muse. I've finally been able to write something that isn't utter garbage.

Chapter Nine

Jutel

Who knew that a man as pompous and self-centered as Kisho could be that good with children? Jutel did her best to put it from her mind and focus on the task at hand. They'd somehow managed to get to the space junk before anyone else and now she was working their tractor beam to pull the prime pieces in, it was precision work and went against what the beam was usually used for. Normally you would latch onto something larger, not lots of little things.

Mal was sitting behind her monitoring the ships systems as she worked. Neither had said anything about Dido and her baby or Kisho and the Venedians after him. Jutel wasn't sure what to say.

"Why do you think Bill brought her?"

Well, Mal seemed to want to talk. Squinting at the screen Jutel concentrated on what she was doing and made a noncommittal noise, which was all he usually needed from her. Mal was—shy, but once he got to know you he wouldn't shut up. He was a fount of useless knowledge with some interesting and useful

stuff thrown in as well and once he latched onto
something he had to know it all.

"I mean who shows up with a woman and a
baby. Do you think the baby's his? He has always
traveled a lot and who knows if they taught safe sex on
Olovia though he probably got that talk on Nian. I
wonder, what's going on there?"

Tuning him out Jutel slowly moved the last bit
of junk into their hold. It was a tight fit and for the first
time ever their cargo bay was filled to the max, but she
hadn't wanted to leave anything behind. Zeke was
doing them a huge favor by sending this job to them
and she didn't want him to regret it.

Ten minutes later Mal was still talking and Jutel
was finishing up. Sighing she leaned back and rubbed
her forehead where a headache had grown. She was
going to have to take a blocker.

Standing up she said, "Can you plot a course to
Andove, I'm going to head to my cabin and get some
rest."

"Sure, I'll set the autopilot and then check on
our guests. Let me know if you need anything else."

She gave him a small smile before leaving. He
knew that something was wrong with her, he was
forever asking her if there was anything he could do,
but she didn't know what to tell him. Become a leader
and give her a new life goal?

That was mean. It wasn't his fault that they'd
failed and he was doing everything he could to help her
out.

In a foul mood and unable to pull herself out of
it Jutel just wanted to get to her room and go to sleep.
At least, while she slept she didn't have to worry about
the future.

"You, it's all your fault. I was doing just fine until you shot me. Now I can't even enjoy a sonic shower without—well I just can't enjoy it anymore."

Walking down the hallway, just wanting to get to her cabin, Kisho had burst out of his room and was shaking his finger at her. He looked flustered. He was still underweight, but an idea struck Jutel. Cocking her head to the side she blocked out the words that were spewing out of his mouth and made her decision.

"Alright, I'll have sex with you."

That shut him up—for a minute.

"What? I mean of course you will, I'd planned on us having sex, I just expected to have to spend more time wooing you. You strike me as the kind that requires a lot of foreplay."

"Nope. I'm pretty much ready to go right now. It's been too long and while normally I wouldn't choose you, you're all that's available."

His jaw dropped before he snapped it shut and said, "What about Mal, surely he would jump at the opportunity to sleep with you."

She snorted, "Mal's gay, I don't have the equipment he wants. Are you gay? Is that why we aren't doing this? If you are just let me know, I can take care of myself all on my own."

She waited for him to respond but when he didn't she side stepped him and went to her room. Closing the door she sighed, it had been worth a shot. She wasn't overly attracted to Kisho, he was going to wind up being a load of trouble she didn't want, but the thought of having sex had been pleasant. She enjoyed receiving pleasure from someone and she'd never been short on partners. Of course on Nian, there were almost four men to every woman so that wasn't saying anything.

Stripping off her uniform she threw it into the cleaning drawer, then grabbed a blocker to fight the headache hammering against her skull. Dimming the lights she lay down and closed her eyes, willing sleep to take over.

A pounding on her door startled her just as she was about to fall asleep. Grumbling she slowly sat up and felt around in the darkness for her robe. The pounding increased. Annoyed she stormed to the door, naked, and keyed it open.

Kisho stood on the other side, his mouth open like he was about to say something, but no words came out. She crossed her arms over her breasts and said, "Are you aware that the doors have chimes? You don't have to knock on it. In fact, I would appreciate it if you didn't. Now, what do you want?"

"You."

He stepped forward, moving his body to hers, his hand going to her cheek, bringing their lips together. It only took a second for Jutel to respond. She backed them into her room and blindly keyed the door closed.

His hands were everywhere and her body was revved up and ready to go instantly. She moved her hand to the waist of his pants and began undoing the snaps.

"Hold on a minute, let's take this slow, I prefer a seduction."

For all of a second, she considered what he was saying, before she shook her head and said, "We do this now or not at all. I'm not looking for a seduction or a relationship or whatever it is you're used to. You've got a clean bill of health, I've got a clean bill of health, let's do this and get back to our lives."

"Really? No foreplay? No flirtations? Just wham, bam, thank you ma'am we're over?"

"Exactly."

He grinned and his eyes sparkled. "I can get used to that."

Jutel stepped back and raised her hand. "Let's get something straight first, this is not something you should get used to. We'll do this now, maybe again, but it's not going to become a routine. We are not going to become an 'item' or whatever title you prefer. So, please, do your best not to fall in love with me, okay? It will just make things awkward."

He looked completely offended by what she'd said and for a moment Jutel thought about apologizing for her bluntness but then he said, "I fall in love with you? I fear my dear Jutel that you've forgotten who I am yet again. I am a prince and not to brag, but I'm the rightful heir to the Venedian throne. If anyone is going to fall in love it's going to be you, so please try and refrain, a broken heart doesn't look good on anyone."

Stepping forward she grabbed the front of his shirt and said, "I'm so glad we've got that out of the way. Now, let's get back to business."

Their lips reconnected, their tongues explored, Jutel nibbled on his bottom lip. Returning to his pants she had them undone and off in a matter of seconds, she didn't bother with his shirt.

Moving back to the bed she tried to push him onto it but he stopped her. Grinning he said, "I prefer to taste the merchandise before I continue."

She was completely fine with that. Lying back on the bed she hoped that Kisho was up to the task, if not she could probably teach him a few things.

His head between her legs was enough to cause

a flood of heat straight to her core. She'd been ready when she'd opened the door, now her body was close to begging for a release.

Her eyes drifted closed as his fingers parted her wet lips, his thumb began circling her sensitive clit and then his tongue. Her eyes flew open when his tongue touched her, she'd had no idea that Venedians had tongues that long, and thick, and dear god he was about to bring her to climax.

Moaning her body bucked against her will, pleasure flooded her body, and Kisho's name slipped from her lips.

He brought his head up, licked his lips, and made a satisfying sound. Only then did he cover her body with his own, she could feel his shaft at her entrance, ready to penetrate. She wrapped her leg around his and rolled them, putting herself on top. After his display, she didn't want to give him any more power.

He grinned up at her. Taking her swaying breasts in his hands he began massaging them while she worked her pussy over his cock. She was more than ready to go again and his stiff length let her know that he was ready as well, but she wanted to wait until the absolute last minute. Taking his cock in her firm grasp she used him. Brushing him against herself, pumping him until he let out a small gasp. That's when she knew.

Straddling Kisho she plunged herself down onto his rock hard cock, taking him all the way to the hilt. She could feel his hands go to her hip as she began rocking there. Slowly she moved herself up. Leaving the fullness his cock, until she plunged back down. She found a rhythm and slowly accelerated it.

She leaned forward and that's when his cock

started rubbing just the right spot. Her pace quickened until her mind went blank and she saw stars. Her orgasm pulsed through her body and she heard Kisho groan at his own release. That was exactly what she'd needed.

Bill's Journal

Dido is not what I expected from my vision. She has almost no mothering instinct, which is fine, of course, but odd based on my own observations. Maybe Venedians don't bond well with babies?

It doesn't matter, I've had more than enough experience and I've been able to take care of her child while she recoups from her ordeal. I've managed to work out what she's been through based on little slips she's made. She seems like a very proud woman but she needs someone to take care of her. That's my specialty.

Still no new visions. It's nice.

Chapter Ten

Kisho

Kisho couldn't keep the grin from his face. He had no idea it was going to be so easy to get Jutel into bed. If he'd known, he would have tried sooner. He conveniently forgot that she was the one that had approached him and that it had nothing to do with his universe renowned charms and everything to do with convenience.

Maybe he hadn't forgotten that completely, but it wasn't important. He was in her bed now and he'd given her not one, but at least two orgasms. Surely now she'd stop shooting him with that awful weapon of hers and maybe he'd rethink stealing her ship.

"So I was thinking," he waited for her to say something snippy or just cut him off with a blatant no, but she didn't so he continued, "I was thinking that we should head to Vende. I've got some business to handle there and I'm sure Mal would enjoy seeing it."

She let out a deep contented sigh and he felt smug. He knew she'd agree to whatever he asked after how he'd just rocked her world. When she moved away from where she'd been cuddled at his side he started to worry. When she raised the lights and he saw her frown he knew something was wrong.

Walking across the room, still very much naked, she grabbed a robe tossed over a large plush chair in the corner. Putting it on she turned to him and said, "We're on our way to Andove, the cargo hold is full of space debris that needs to go there. Once we've talked with our contact there, then we'll talk, but I don't see it happening. We barely have enough money for such a long trip. If you need to go to Vende then maybe you'll be able to find someone there that will take you."

Propping himself up on his elbow Kisho put on his most charming smile and said, "Not even after all I've given you? I promise that wasn't the last of it, we've barely scratched the surface of my sexual abilities."

Her back went ramrod straight and he knew immediately that he'd said something wrong, but for the life of him, he couldn't figure out what. She walked to the door, keyed it open, and said, "I'd like you to leave now."

He threw off the sheet so that she could get an eyeful of his naked body, but she didn't give in. If anything her frown deepened and she seemed somehow angrier. He knew the pleasure points on twenty-five female species, he'd made an Eloian scream out in ecstasy during the month of silence, he'd taken part in several sanctioned orgies and each of his partners had given him high marks. All of that and he still didn't understand women.

Grumbling he stood up, put his clothes on, and left the room. The door slid shut as soon as he was over the threshold. Standing in the corridor he decided to take a walk through the ship while he decided what to do next.

He had to get to Vende. He had the proof he needed now. The only way he was going to get his cousin to pay up was to approach the head magistrate with his proof. A quiet contract could be negotiated and Kisho could take the money and retire. He'd live out his life on Ostara or some other planet like that, maybe one less crowded. Hell, maybe he'd make enough to buy his own planet, that would be something.

First, though, he had to get to Vende. He found himself walking toward the cockpit. It would be very easy to re-route their current trip. Ostara was only about a week away from Vende. He wasn't even sure where Andove was, so who knew how long it would take him once he got there. Unfortunately, Mal was sitting in the cockpit a tablet in his hands, reading whatever was on it. When he heard Kisho his head came up but for once he didn't say anything.

Making a decision to feel him out for options Kisho sat down on the free seat and said, "So you're gay? I didn't know that. Is that why you've been talking to me so much? I've had my share of male on male, and I'm not opposed to it, but I'm currently going through a female kick. Give me a few months, though, and I'm sure I'll swing back."

Mal's eyes bugged out and his jaw dropped. Kisho smiled, he had that effect on men. The minute they found out he was open to that direction it was like a kid on Christmas, they lost all ability to talk and could only imagine the possibilities. It really was a blessing that his parents had only had him. Imagine if there was more than one of him roaming the universe.

Well—let's just say the Nians wouldn't be experiencing a population crisis that's for sure.

Mal stuttered, "Wh-what are you—you're crazy! H-h-how could you—what?!"

Intrigued Kisho said, "Oh was Jutel wrong? Are you not? I wonder where she got that idea?"

Agitated Mal stood up, then sat back down, then stood up again. He eventually settled on pacing in the tight quarters, his movements jerky and his ears a deep red. "I-I-I never told her I was gay. I'm not gay. Not that there's a problem with that, you can sleep with whoever you want I don't care, I'm not going to judge, but seriously why would she think that? I mean—I—"

His words stopped making sense and Kisho started to grow bored. Checking his fingernails he said, "Are you in love with her? Is that why you're so surprised? Has she put you in the friend zone and your heart pines for what you can't have?"

Mal shot him a dirty look before throwing himself back down on the chair. "Don't be stupid, Jutel is like a sister to me. I don't know why she thought—that she thought I was gay just seems—"

"Has she seen you with other women?"

"I come from a planet with a serious lack of females. Hell I went to Earth to find one, why would she think—it doesn't make sense. Whatever, I'll just—it doesn't matter. I'm not interested in her, I've never been interested in her, like I said she's basically the sister I never had. I'm just surprised she would jump to that conclusion. I mean, yeah, I have some weird interests, but that doesn't mean anything in this day and age. It's not like we're from Earth were people believe in those stereotypes. I just—"

He stood up again and Kisho raised his hands

in mock surrender, "Hey, I get it, no one likes to be misjudged, but you're kidding yourself if you think only people on some planet I've never heard of judge people based on stereotypes. In my travels I've found that happens on all planets, the only difference is what the stereotype is. On some planets it might be considered super macho to be obsessed with cultural facts and societal norms or whatever it was you've been talking to me about these last few days. I haven't been to that planet, but that doesn't mean it's not out there."

Mal glared at him and crossed his arms before sitting back down. He swiveled the chair so that his back was to Kisho and he didn't say another word. Taking his cue, and realizing that he wasn't going to be able to change the course with Mal sitting right there, Kisho got up and left.

The ship was small and he'd already explored every available inch of it, but he couldn't just go back to his cabin. He was restless and jumpy. He'd come very close to getting arrested and then after his all too brief liaison with Jutel he wasn't ready to go to sleep, even though the ships internal clock showed evening hours.

Frowning, Kisho shoved his hands in his pockets and walked toward the cargo bay. He looked at the piles of junk that were waiting and wondered if he could just jettison it so they could get on their way to Vende. Even he wasn't clueless enough to think Jutel would let him get by with that. Nian or not she'd probably jettison him right along with it.

He muttered under his breath about women and how they were only good for one thing, that was the only reason that Bill was able to sneak up on him.

"It's probably not a good idea to send the junk out into space, no matter how attractive the thought is."

Kisho jumped, startled by Bill's voice. Turning to the boy he tried to appear as though that wasn't exactly what he was thinking but something about this kid saw right through him. Knowing when he was caught he grinned and said, "I'd already decided not to do it. I figure once Jutel found out I'd be right behind it."

"She probably wouldn't do that, but she'd want to. You'll get to Vende, just give it some time."

Frowning Kisho said, "How did you know that's what I wanted to do? Have you been talking to Jutel?"

Bill gave him an enigmatic smile that sent a chill down Kisho's spine. There was something about Bill, but he couldn't put his finger on it. There were the odd predictions said with absolute authority, but there had to be something else. He'd met plenty of people who thought they had a good enough handle on people that they could predict their actions. They were cocky, but Bill didn't seem that way. He was different and that's what concerned Kisho.

"So what do you think I should do? You know Jutel better than I do, how can I get her to take me to Vende?"

Sighing Bill dropped his gaze and all of a sudden he was no longer a mysterious figure, but a young man that seemed unsure about the future.

"Normally I could tell you exactly what you would do, but—there are too many unknowns. Dido and her baby confuse things, I can't see—I don't know. Be nice, don't bug her, be helpful, Jutel likes helping people even if she doesn't believe that right now. Just—be careful with her. She's—confused right now, she needs a purpose. Do you think you could give her a purpose?"

Grinning now Kisho wiggled his eyebrows when he said, "Oh I can give her a purpose alright."

Bill didn't understand at first then laughed. "I don't think she'll accept that, but you could certainly try, it will be very amusing. I'll be in my cabin if you decide to take that approach, let me know so I can watch."

Kinky. Not what he expected at all from the young man, but it takes all kinds. Bill left and Kisho continued to stare at the space debris for a few more minutes before going back to his own cabin. He was no closer to an answer, but he was tired and didn't see the point in forcing an idea. His best always came after a refreshing sleep, which was preceded by passionate lovemaking. Hopefully, his romp with Jutel was passionate enough to get his creative juices flowing.

Mal's Notes

For some reason Jutel thinks I'm gay. I had no idea until Kisho mentioned it. Maybe he was just messing with me?

Whatever, it doesn't matter. All it does is prove it's been too long since I've been with a woman. Like I needed that reminder. Nian was a bust, Earth was a bust, and so far the universe hasn't given me the opportunity to find my partner.

Maybe I should talk with Jutel. Ask her to find a planet for us to stay on for a while. Benjo was nice. Maybe I could find my blond bombshell and we could make beautiful babies together.

It's not like I don't want a family. I do. I just haven't had the opportunity that apparently Kisho has.

Once the salvage is dropped and we figure out what to do with Dido maybe I can convince Jutel to find a planet. In the meantime, I'm just going to continue channeling my frustrations into my story.

Chapter Eleven

Jutel

Jutel woke up feeling refreshed. Her headache was gone and her body felt limber. Even though she was more than a little annoyed at how things had ended with Kisho, she was happy that she'd gotten what she needed from him. In fact, as long as he could remember she wasn't at his beck and call, she could easily see herself inviting him back to her bed. She'd give him some time to stew, first. She didn't want him to think that she needed him, he just happened to have something she wanted.

Getting dressed she decided to head up to the cockpit and work on the problems currently circling her brain.

"I'm not gay. I just want to clear that up. Why did you even—never mind it's not important. I'm not attracted to you if that's what you're thinking. I just wanted to clear that up also. Kisho mentioned that you said I was and I'm not so I just thought that I would set you straight. So—you know—if you see any hot alien women just point them my way—cause I'm totally into all that and—I'm going to go now."

Jutel felt blindsided. She'd been walking down the crew's quarter's corridor when Mal had met her. He'd seemed annoyed but by the time he'd finished his poorly thought out statement his ears had been flaming and his eyes wouldn't meet hers. It was a level of awkward she'd never seen him achieve before and she'd seen some pretty uncomfortable displays.

When he left she stood there for a moment and contemplated what to do. She was tempted to seek out Kisho and yell at him for making her live through that, but just the idea of going to Kisho was enough to remind her of his request and piss her off all over again. You have sex with a man just once and then he immediately starts trying to take advantage of the situation. It's not like she'd been crystal clear about what she expected from the exchange.

Really, though, what had she expected? He was Kisho and even though she'd only known him a couple days she was fairly certain she could predict his actions one hundred percent of the time. In fact, she predicted right now that if he hadn't retired to his cabin he would be up in the unattended cockpit trying to reroute their trip. Of course, he didn't know about the safety measures put into place to keep that from happening, but she doubted they would stop him from trying.

What was she going to do about him?

Peeking in on Dido and her baby she found the two of them asleep. Bill must have gone back to his own room because they were alone. Making as little noise as possible she left them alone and made her way up to the cockpit. She had a lot she needed to figure out.

Sitting in the captain's chair she pulled up an

old to-do list she'd created. At the beginning of their year of space travel it had helped remind her to do certain things. Now they were either all automated or second nature so she hadn't used it in a while. Deleting what had been there she looked at the empty line after the number one and hesitated before typing, Take Debris to Zeke. That really was their number one priority right now.

The next item on the list was complicated, should it be Dido or Kisho? Kisho was clearly wanted by the Venedians and she didn't like hiding a fugitive. On the other hand, she found it difficult to believe that he'd done something truly awful. He was harmless and seemed barely capable of taking care of himself, let alone managing to harm someone.

Item two, find out what Kisho did, which then made item three, find out more about Dido.

Sighing she leaned back and looked at the list. It was basic and not really helpful, but it did give her some place to start. Closing it she opened another screen and started searching the universal data stream for information on Kisho. She started with Vende and went from there. It made for boring reading, though she assumed Mal would have loved to do it if he hadn't done so already. After their brief meeting in the hall, though, she didn't feel like approaching him.

After two hours her eyes started to ache and she closed the screen and stood up. She didn't know if she'd learned anything helpful, but she, at least, knew more about Vende than she had. Checking their progress to Andove she headed to the cargo bay only to remember that it was full of junk and she couldn't use it to exercise.

"Stupid, you literally just checked the course,

how could you forget that stuff was there?"

She barely stopped herself from replying to her own question, but it was close. Rubbing her forehead she tried to come up with an alternative to running a holo suite exercise program. As if summoned Kisho appeared and he gave her a knowing smile, which was the wrong thing to do.

Glaring she turned away from him and stomped to her cabin. Like she was going to give him the satisfaction? The man was ridiculous. She should never have had sex with him because now he was going to think he had some kind of power of her. As if she could be that easy.

Fuming and stuck in her room Jutel started doing the only exercise she could in the close quarters. It wasn't much, barely more than push up and sit ups, but it was better than seeking out Kisho.

She was at it for over an hour when her personal comm unit dinged letting her know that there was movement from Dido's cabin. Grabbing a towel she dabbed at the sweat she'd managed to work up and debated whether or not she should take a shower first. Shrugging her shoulders Jutel decided she hadn't worked up that much of sweat and she really needed information if she was going to figure out what they were going to do.

Stepping out of her cabin Jutel found Dido standing in the hallway an odd look on her face. Her eyes darted to Jutel's then dropped and she started back toward her cabin.

"Hey, is there anything I can help you with? Do you need food? Did Bill give you any?"

Dido hesitated and her hands twisted in front of her. Her voice was soft when she finally spoke, "I was wondering if you could tell me how the shower works. Bill mentioned that it was sonic, but—I don't know what that means. The baby is fed and sleeping and I thought I could take a shower before she wakes up again."

Jutel tried to put a warm and helpful smile on her face when she said, "Why don't I show you how it works in my cabin, that way we don't wake the baby. All the rooms are pretty much the same, so the showers work the same way."

Dido hesitated and Jutel tried to appear as non-threatening as possible, which was not something she usually tried to do. It must have worked because Dido rewarded her with a tentative smile and took a step toward her.

It didn't take long, the shower was idiot proof, and Jutel assured her that she wasn't going to break anything. Dido seemed terrified at that prospect.

"I just—I don't—Bill said it wouldn't be a problem, but I don't have any money and I couldn't afford to replace anything and—I've never been on a ship this nice before."

Her head dropped and Jutel tried to think of something to say. She really should have pumped Bill for information before confronting Dido. "You're not going to break anything and if you do it's no big deal."

She paused before continuing, unsure if her questions would cause Dido to feel unwelcome, but she needed to know more. Tugging on her ear she activated her implants before she said, "If you don't mind my asking, why did you leave Benjo? It seemed like a nice planet, what we saw of it."

Dido's heart rate skyrockets and her hands went back to being twisted in front of her. A sinking feeling hit Jutel's stomach, she knew whatever was about to come was probably not good.

Dido's eyes wouldn't meet Jutel's and her words came out rushed. "I'm a slave. My new master was reviewing some property he owned on Benjo, that's where I gave birth. He—he wanted me to give up my baby. He was mad that she was a girl, he said that—he—I was running away. I knew I shouldn't, that it was just going to get me in trouble, but I couldn't leave my baby, I couldn't do it, and I was hoping that someone would help me or—Bill said that you would take care of us. That everything would be okay. He found me hiding behind a crate of rations—I—please don't be mad at him. He was just being nice and—He said that you would help and I was so afraid and I know I should have said something earlier but—I'm sorry please don't hurt us."

She cringed in front of Jutel, waiting for a blow, and it took all of Jutel's strength not to snap. After what she'd seen on Olovia where they'd found Bill, slavery was one of her triggers. She had a pretty level head and rarely lost her temper, even though she was perpetually pissed off, but seeing those that were weaker being taken advantage of in that way could cause her to destroy buildings.

None of that mattered right now, though, because there was a woman in front of her who was terrified and hurt and truly believed that she was about to be beaten for doing what came natural, trying to save her child.

Jutel tried to hide all that she was feeling so that none of it came through in her voice when she said, "Dido we would be happy to help you. We'll do everything we can to keep you and your daughter safe.

You don't have anything to fear while you're on this ship, I promise you."

Dido met her gaze briefly before dropping her eyes again. She nodded her head and mumbled that she was going to go back to her cabin now. Jutel didn't stop her. Standing in the middle of her room, she took deep breaths to try and suppress the rage boiling inside of her. A noise brought her eyes to the doorway and she saw Kisho standing there. He wasn't doing as good a job hiding his emotions.

The sound of Dido's cabin door closing met their ears and his voice was thick with fury when he said, "There's a special place in hell for slavers and slave-owners."

She walked forward and keyed her door closed, locking him out. She wasn't capable of dealing with an empathetic Kisho right now. It made things easier for her if she didn't like him.

Bill's Journal

The tension between Jutel and Kisho would be amusing if I wasn't so distracted. Dido is like no woman I've ever been around. She's delicate and helpless, but strong and courageous. She's escaped her captors, saving her daughter from the same life, and yet she's unable to complete basic tasks.

She's a study in contrasts and I'm greatly enjoying my time with her and her child. Nothing else matters right now, only them.

I should probably tell Jutel about my visions, or lack thereof.

Chapter Twelve

Kisho

Kisho frowned at the closed door, before turning around and heading back to his cabin. He'd only left because his comm had alerted him that someone was in the hallway like he'd programmed it to. He'd listened as Jutel had taught Dido how to use the shower stall and waited for his opportunity to jump in, he hadn't been expecting Dido's revelation. It struck a nerve.

He was many things and he was honest, with himself, so he was fine admitting them. He was a thief, often times a bad one. He was a liar, he could be manipulative if the situation arose, and he had an obsession with making a large sum of money. All that, though, and he'd never had to enslave someone, he'd never killed anyone, he'd never even put someone in a bad situation they'd be unable to recover from. Sure he thought about stealing The Flower, but he hadn't done it yet. Not because he couldn't, cause he totally could, but because he was starting to realize that it was all Jutel, Mal, and Bill had and they were turning out to be alright people.

Annoying people, but still alright.

Lying down on his bed he stared up at the plain white ceiling of his cabin and tried to forget what he'd overheard. He had other things he needed to be thinking about instead of the plight of a very large portion of the galaxy that he couldn't help.

His comm chimed again letting him know someone was in the hallway. His eyes darted to the door before he stood up and keyed it open. He stood off to the side so that whoever was out there couldn't see him.

Eavesdropping was considered by some a bad habit. You could hear some very unflattering things, but Kisho didn't look at it that way. Sure he'd overheard more than one conversation about how much a bastard he was or how stupid he was, but he'd also gotten some vital intelligence that way so he discarded the negative and continued the habit.

He heard pacing and when he strained his ears he heard another door slide open.

"What do you want Bill? I'm not in the mood for a vague glimpse of the future right now."

"That's just it, I can't see the future."

There was a moment of silence before Jutel said, "What do you mean?"

She sounded concerned but Bill seemed gleeful when he said, "When we were on Benjo in that store, right before I found Dido, I discovered that I couldn't see the future anymore."

"Has that ever happened?"

"No. Well, I've never been able to see my own future very well, but I've never had a total blackout like this before."

"So it's total? You can't see anything?"

"Nothing, well, mostly nothing. Every now and then I get some flashes but they're hazy like when it's something that has a low probability of happening."

"What could this mean?"

"I don't know."

There was a longer stretch of silence and then Jutel said, "Let me know if it changes."

"Of course."

Kisho heard footsteps walk down the hall, pause at his open doorway, then move past.

Well that was new. Who knew that there was another psychic race out there? That could be some very valuable information, to the right person it could be positively priceless. Filing it away he wondered if he should try and visit Jutel again, give her a purpose in life.

He grinned at the prospect and swung his feet off the bed and stood up. There was a small square mirror on the wall, it was basically useless since he couldn't see his entire body, but a glance at it told him he was as devilishly handsome as ever. She may have closed the door in his face earlier, but that wasn't going to happen this time.

Swaggering out of his room he nearly collided with the woman of his thoughts. She frowned at him and his smile grew, she was so adorable.

"Stop eavesdropping."

"But I learn such interesting things. I could have done without the reminder of the more disgusting parts of our universe, but oh well, I can't always hear pleasant things. Speaking of pleasant, I was thinking— your place or mine this time?"

Her face was blank and he truly had no idea if she was about to take him up on the offer or blast him with her cannon again. He started to fidget, something he never did, but the idea of that cannon was enough to make any man fear.

Finally, Jutel said, "Yours." She pushed him back into his room and keyed the door closed. She didn't bother with her top, which was really a shame since her breasts were truly wondrous and he'd yet to really get to pay them the attention they deserved. But if she wanted to be quick, he could do that too.

If she wasn't going to take off all her clothes then he wouldn't take off any. Undoing the flap at the front of his pants he pulled out his already hard cock. He backed her up against the wall took one of her legs and wrapped it around his waist, that put her right where he needed her. She wrapped her arms around his neck while he took his cock in his hand and guided it to her wet pussy. That was one of the things he was starting to like about her, she was always ready for him.

She wanted quick so that's what he was going to give her. He thrust into her in one swift movement. Her velvety softness surrounded him and it would have been all too easy to just cum right then, but quick and unsatisfying were two separate things.

Her nails dug into his back through his shirt and she let out a groan that had him pulling out then moving right back in. She brought her other leg up and dug her heels into his backside, urging him to go faster.

Kisho thrust into her over and over until he felt her clench around him, she let out a satisfied moan and he finally let himself go. Feeling flushed and satisfied, all though a little bit miffed at the speed of everything, he backed up and slowly let her down. They cleaned up silently and he could tell she was about to leave so he opened his mouth and apparently put his foot right in.

"So how about making that your purpose in life? I mean, it wouldn't last forever, I'm not the staying kind, but for a time at least."

Her gaze was hooded when she turned around and said, "Excuse me?"

Realizing he'd bungled the delivery and probably shouldn't have used the whole 'purpose in life' phrase, Kisho tried to fix it and said, "What I mean is, how about you be on call for me day and night. Any time I have an itch it'll get satisfied. I mean, if you have an itch we could work something out as well, of course, I'm more than willing to satisfy your needs. What else are we going to do on this trip? It's not like you've got any entertainment with the cargo bay full. This way we can have some fun and the trip won't be so depressing. How about it?"

Her voice was low when she spoke, each word hitting him like the sharp sting of a laser pistol. A cold sweat broke across his brow as an evolutionary defense mechanism kicked in. The only thing keeping him from running was the fact that she blocked his path to freedom.

"My purpose in life? You want to be *my* purpose in life? Well doesn't that sound peachy? I should thank you, I've felt aimless for a while, but now that I have a *purpose* I'm all better. Tell me *Prince* Kisho what exactly can I do for you today? Do you have an itch right now that I can satisfy? Would you like me to get on my knees and pleasure you with my tongue? Maybe I should just bend over so you can have your way with my ass.

"What made you think that I don't have a purpose? That I need *you* to give me one? You know what? I don't care, but let me make it abundantly clear, if you *ever* feel the need to give me a *purpose* you can take that seed of a thought and shove it so far up your ass that you choke. Do I make myself clear?"

Was it unmanly that he didn't trust himself to speak so only nodded?

Her eyes were cold and the temperature in the room seemed to drop several degrees as she held his gaze until he couldn't meet it. She stood there a moment longer before turning and leaving his cabin. Kisho didn't leave his room for the next twenty-four hours and the only reason he left then was he'd run out of rations.

When Bill saw him he said, "Dude, I told you to ask her while I was watching."

Bill and Mal roared with laughter until tears came to their eyes. Every time they seemed like they were about to stop they'd look at him and start all over again.

The whole damn crew was crazy.

Mal's Notes

I wish I'd seen Jutel tell off Kisho, it would have been great for my story. Still, I think I'll be able to relay the gist of it fairly well. I'm making good progress, which is understandable considering I'm surrounded by inspiration.

There's something clearly going on between Jutel and Kisho and I think that Bill has feelings for Dido. It looks like I'm, again, the odd man out. Trying not to dwell on it.

I made a list of soap opera clichés that I love, I'm going to try and work them ALL into my story. We'll see what happens, I don't want to be too heavy-handed.

-Evil Twin
-Death Bed Declaration
-Medical Miracle
-Bring someone back to life

Chapter Thirteen

Jutel

Two weeks of ignoring Kisho sped by, it was really easy to do and oddly incredibly satisfying. By the time it was over Jutel felt rejuvenated. She was filled with such a righteous indignation whenever she saw his stupid face that the apathy and depression she'd been experiencing was gone. He'd tried to give her a purpose and she'd found one in hating him. It was petty but oh so fulfilling and a perfect way to pass the time.

Of course, she couldn't help but notice how well he'd started to fill out his clothes and the memories of their first time having sex still sent delicious shivers down her spine. It would almost be worth it to figure out what he could do to her body. Almost.

"Please land in docking bay two."

Jutel guided The Flower into the station and breathed a sigh of relief. They'd made it to Andove with the cargo intact. Things had started out a little rocky, but it had been smooth sailing at the end.

When she disembarked Zeke was waiting for her, but he wasn't smiling, which was odd. Zeke was almost always smiling. He was a very happy guy, especially when his wife, Anika, was around. Normally she was right by his side when Jutel disembarked but she was nowhere to be seen this time.

"Jutel, how was the trip?"

She gave him a small smile, "It went fine. Sorry it took so long we had to stop and get supplies before we could pick up the stock. Plus, you know, it wasn't actually close. I was surprised that you guys were hauling out so far."

He didn't return her smile and Jutel started to grow concerned.

"We've been searching further out, the business is booming and there's a lot of competition, both on planet and off."

"Of course."

"Did you pick up anyone on your way here? When you stopped for supplies?"

His eyes bored into hers and she felt goosebumps pop up on her arm. Something wasn't right. Tugging on her ear she activated her implants and data started streaming in front of her. Zeke's heart rate was elevated, which was never a good thing for a shifter. There was also no one on the dock unloading the cargo.

Kisho, it had to be Kisho, what had he done? She should have spent time interrogating him instead of enjoying being angry.

"What do you mean Zeke? You've known me how long? When have I ever had anyone other than Mal and Bill?"

Zeke didn't react to Bill's name, which said a lot since he'd never met or even heard of him. She didn't know why, but something was telling her that she shouldn't mention who else was on the ship. She certainly didn't owe Kisho anything or even Dido and her daughter for that matter, but they were crew. She protected her crew, even when she wasn't sure why.

"Jutel, I'm going to have to ask you to tell your crew to disembark. It's strictly for security measures, I'm sure you understand."

Giving a slight nod Jutel said, "Oh course Zeke, you've always been a friend, whatever you think is best."

She slowly took out her comm, making it as visible as possible, but she noticed the tension in Zeke's face ratchet up when she made the move. She was incredibly thankful that she'd strapped her cannon to her leg, but she didn't want anyone that could be watching to think that's where she was headed.

"Hey Mal, I need the *crew* to disembark."

There was a pause and Jutel held her breath until Mal answered, "The crew? Are you serious? Bill and I are a crew now? Okay, sure."

She had to resist the urge to breathe a sigh of relief so thankful that Mal had detected her subtle wording. As long as Dido, the baby, and Kisho could stay silent and hide hopefully they would make it out in one piece. Then she'd try and figure out what was going on with Zeke.

Mal and Bill disembarked and Zeke gave them a visual once over before saying, "This is it? You don't have anyone else?"

"Well we had picked up someone right before I talked to you, but they got off when we stopped for supplies. Who exactly are you looking for? We aren't bounty hunters, but honestly at this point, I wouldn't be against it."

Zeke glanced over his shoulder and a man in a United Universe Aid Coalition uniform came walking toward them. Right behind him were a group of Zeke's employees holding the transport equipment they used. It was a version of a teleporter, it required them to set up beacons around the cargo, but then it was all easily teleported to a sorter.

The UUAC officer ignored the workers and went straight to Jutel. He didn't even acknowledge Zeke before saying, "Jutel of Nian, do you have any other designation?"

"No, that works fine."

"I show that your DNA is on file with us, I need to verify your identity now."

He didn't ask, just reached out and pressed a scanner to her shoulder. A needle poked through her arm and took a blood sample. She didn't move even though instinct had her wanting to lash out. She knew that her nanites wouldn't show up on the scan and the UUAC didn't know she had bio-implants so she was still at an advantage. Those were both things she'd conveniently forgotten to mention when she'd applied her planet for a position on their council. Maybe if she'd shared that particular Nian capability she could have secured a spot, but she doubted it. The UUAC wasn't what she'd imagined and even though she hadn't seen this coming it wasn't all together surprising.

The officer did the same test for Mal and Bill and waited for the information to confirm. When it did he seemed more at ease. He put the scanner away and looked at Jutel. "I'm sure you understand. The Emperor of Vende has recently suffered a personal loss, a—female servant of his has gone missing. He was very fond of this—servant and would like her back.

You left Benjo right before she was discovered missing and we were unable to contact you during your trip, though many attempts were made."

Jutel dipped her head and barely resisted the urge to clench her fists. Servant? Really? Slavery was supposed to be illegal in the UUAC, but then so were a lot of things. If you were certain member planets they let you get away with a lot.

"I apologize, our ship is small, and doesn't have the best communications. If I had known I would of course gone to the closest UUAC location. Our ship was searched before we left Benjo for a passenger we'd transported, but I wasn't aware there was also a missing servant. I hope that you find her soon and in good care."

The officer had already dismissed Jutel and wasn't paying attention to what she was saying. Instead, he was eyeing her ship in appreciation. Her eyes darted to Zeke who was still on edge but looked in better control. His eyes hadn't changed so that was a good sign.

Finally, the officer turned back to her and said, "I'm Captain Fah if you ever feel like selling that ship let me know. I would make it worth your while."

Putting her best fake smile on Jutel said, "Thank you, but The Flower was specifically made for me by my people and I don't see myself parting with it."

Captain Fah nodded his head in understanding and thankfully didn't push the issue before striding away from the dock, leaving Zeke, Jutel, and both their crews. Jutel opened her mouth to ask what the hell was going on, but Zeke stopped her with a lifted finger and shook his head.

She bit her tongue and waited, hoping that they would get an opportunity to speak soon. Mal and Bill shared a look with her, but neither of them said anything. They all stood in silence as the cargo bay of The Flower was emptied and Zeke's crew left the dock.

Zeke turned to Jutel and said, "Not here, if you can port to my home I can talk there. Your people will be fine on your ship, it's being scanned by the UUAC so it shouldn't be searched. I'm sorry for all this—I—we'll talk later."

He followed his crew off the dock and Jutel was left with Mal and Bill. "I'll head to his house, you two stay here. I'll let you know as soon as I can what's going on. For now—turtles the word."

She was proud of the fact that the two men didn't give away the code she'd just used. Instead Mal rolled his eyes and said, "Mum, the Earth saying is mums the word and that isn't even the saying you were trying to use. You really need to watch more of the soaps, you'd catch up on the lingo so much faster."

Bill threw his arm over Mal's shoulder and steered him toward the ship while explaining to him that no one in their right mind would choose to watch more Earth soap operas. Jutel had already moved on and was processing what she'd learned so far and what she hoped Zeke could tell her.

Outside of the docking station was a porter, Jutel chose to use it instead of the ships not only because it had Zeke's location already available, but because Andovian porters were much better than Nians. It was something she'd noticed the last time she'd visited, something that she should probably tell the people back on Nian. Not that the porters on Nian were dangerous, but they could stand to have some improvements made.

Jutel's bio-signature was approved for transport directly to Zeke's house. When she materialized Zeke was waiting for her in his home's entryway. Her eyes were unable to resist the impulse and instead of getting right down to business like she should, she stared at the painting behind him on the wall. It was a lone wolf, howling at the moon. Just one moon which was odd since Andove had two. She'd noticed the painting last time she'd been there and it had haunted her.

She was Nian and appreciated art, but it had been a while since a piece had spoken to her like this one. None of that mattered right now, though and she tore her gaze away to stare at Zeke. If anything he seemed more anxious now than he had been. His eyes were glowing which meant his change was very close to the surface. She didn't move, didn't drop her gaze, just waited to see what would happen. Hoping that if need be her draw would be fast enough to access her cannon in case he couldn't control himself and attacked.

"Jutel, I'm sorry, I wish I could have warned you, but—the whole thing has just been a giant cluster fuck. I'm in the middle of a ridiculous feud with a competitor, which is the only reason why I had men out so far in the first place. If I hadn't contacted you—I'm sorry. I never meant to get you mixed up in any of this."

He stopped talking and took a deep breath, then another, slowly bringing himself and his animal side under control. It wasn't until his heart rate calmed that Jutel said, "I think you should start at the beginning, or close to it. How did you get me mixed up in an escaped slave? How is that your fault, exactly?"

His eyes grew wide and he said, "Escaped slave?

I don't know anything about that. I was talking about the whole UUAC thing. They would never have scanned you if I hadn't asked you for help."

Jutel sighed, "Zeke I never realized you had a god complex. You offered me a job because you knew I needed it. I accepted. You did not sick the UUAC on me, they already hate me by the way, and you didn't force me to do anything. Where did this inflated sense of power come from?"

A voice from another room called out, "That's what I said."

Anika entered and smiled at Jutel before moving to stand beside Zeke. She wrapped her arm around his waist and pulled him close to her. Jutel could see the last lines of tension slip from Zeke's shoulders as he took the comfort his mate was offering. He put his arm around her shoulders to complete the picture.

Jutel had to work at not sighing. She was Nian after all, this was the image that was ingrained in her head, the goal she was supposed to achieve, though, normally there would be about four other men in the background. She may not want the numbers, but she wouldn't say no to a partner.

"Jutel, I'm sorry for the less than warm welcome. Why don't you come to the kitchen? I've got some brownies I just pulled out of the oven and there's a stew simmering on the stove."

Zeke grinned down at his wife then at Jutel, "My wife actually cooks, none of that ready-made stuff for us."

Anika rolled her eyes and moved to lead the way. "You know hardly any Andovians use that stuff."

"I know that, but who knows what Nians eat.

They could be like most of the rest of the galaxy and survive on that junk."

Jutel listened to the back and forth and felt a tightening in her stomach. She did her best to ignore it and mostly succeeded.

"Not to be a buzzkill, you two are really adorable, but I need to get back to my ship."

The couple exchanged a worried glance and Zeke said, "Of course. Here sit down, eat, and we'll talk."

Taking her seat Jutel listened as he explained a feud that had started between him and a rival Andovian company. It had started out small, but things were escalating too quickly for his liking. How this tied into Jutel and The Flower she wasn't sure, but she listened as her friend spoke.

"Apparently Pinzan is friends with some people influential in the UUAC and while Andove isn't a member we still feel their influence. I never expected him to go that far, to make up a story and pull in a Captain. It's too much. I think it might be time to bring in the authorities."

Jutel didn't stop the sigh this time. Zeke knew less than she did. She was almost one hundred percent sure that his rival was not the cause for the UUAC visit. She would need to speak with Dido, but she was fairly certain that she was the missing 'servant' though it was still possible Kisho was the cause of all the fuss. It would be so much easier if it was Kisho, she wouldn't have as hard a time dropping him off somewhere. Dido, on the other hand, would weigh on her conscience. She would need to find a safe place for her and the child to hide. Nian maybe?

"Zeke, I'm pretty sure your rival isn't the cause

for the UUAC interference, so I wouldn't go to the authorities about it."

Shocked Zeke said, "Really? Are you sure? Pinzan is a real asshole, he's entirely capable to doing something like this."

"Yeah, I'm pretty sure. I'd tell you more, but I don't want to get you into trouble. In fact, I should probably leave now."

The couple exchanged another worried glance while Jutel stood up and started taking her empty plates to the kitchen area to clean. She waited patiently, even though she didn't have the time, and finally Anika spoke up.

"Zeke, are you sure? Clearly she's got a lot going on, I don't want to—"

He cut her off, "Anika, you know why we're doing this."

Anika's head dropped for a moment then she took a deep breath and nodded her head. "You're right, I know you are, but—he's my baby, I'll always want to protect him."

"You are protecting him, which is why we're doing this."

The two went silent again, exchanging looks of love and Jutel started to worry that things were about to get more complicated for her and her crew.

Zeke squeezed Anika's hand then turned to Jutel and said, "I have a favor to ask, you can of course say no and it's not going to harm our relationship in anyway. I'll still send jobs your way when I can and before I forget I've already transferred your payment for this last shipment into your account."

He stopped and Jutel couldn't keep from saying, "Just come out with it Zeke."

"Right, sorry, it's just—our oldest son, Raiden, is going through some things right now. He's too smart for his own good and if he continues the way he is he's going to end up getting into trouble. Trouble, I can't get him out of. We've tried everything we can, but he's stopped listening to us. Now he's started hanging out with members of Pinzan's clan and we don't know what to do with him anymore."

Zeke paused then rushed on at Jutel's look of concern. "It's not that he's bad, not really, he's a good kid. It's just that he goes about things the wrong way. He's inherited my gift with computer only he's much better than I ever was and he's not getting the right outlets on Andove. We're not a tech planet, we've got our strengths, but they aren't challenging him. I'm just—we're just afraid that he's going to make some bad decisions out of boredom."

"You think my ship is exciting? Most of the time we barely have enough credits to buy food, let alone entertain a boy who's looking for trouble."

Anika shifted on her feet and a low growl came from her throat. Jutel realized she probably shouldn't insult her son, but what did they expect from her? She had an escaped slave, an infant, and a Kisho on her ship already, that was already on top of a man that loved watching drama, made up or not, and a man that could see into the future, only that ability wasn't even working for him right now. Now her friends, people she looked to for help, were asking her to take their troubled son under her wing and what? Knock some sense into him? Show him how the universe really worked?

Rubbing her forehead, Jutel knew that she was going to say yes, she had too. They *were* her friends. They had also helped her out on several occasions, but why did they have to ask for this favor. Couldn't they ask for something else?

Zeke had gone to Anika and was rubbing her shoulders, which seemed to be calming the mama wolf down. Jutel could see that he was going to back down, could already see that defeat in his eyes. He was a strong man, she knew that he'd built his business up from scratch. He'd worked hard and made a name for himself. He and Anika wouldn't have asked unless they didn't see any other option.

"Fine, I'll take him. I can't promise his safety, I'm sorry, I wish I could. I'll do everything in my power to protect him, but as you can see the UUAC are not my friends. I don't think they're my enemy, but things are leaning more that way presently. It's not something I'm trying to do, and I certainly want to avoid trouble, but I won't back down from my beliefs. If you still want him to come with us then have him meet me at the dock in an hour. I'm going to pick up some fresh supplies then head out, unless you have an assignment for me?"

She tried not to look too eager at that last part but still couldn't hide her disappointment when Zeke shook his head no. Oh well, it had been worth a shot. She left the couple in the kitchen and made her way back to their personal porter. She glanced at the painting one more time, taking in the large snowcapped mountains in the distance and the way the wolf stood with purpose even though it was all alone, then stepped into the porter and dematerialized.

Bill's Journal

Andove is a nice planet. I had wanted to show Dido around, but the UUAC reared its ugly head. If my visions were working I would have known that and could have warned Jutel. As is, we're lucky the UUAC's scans can't penetrate the smuggling cubby The Flower has.

If I wasn't so in love I'd be worried about my lack of sight, but Dido distracts me. She is a breath of fresh air and each day with her feels like heaven. She's sweet and soft one minute but can be so grumpy if I interrupt her quiet time.

She still hasn't warmed up to her daughter and I worry about that, but once again I don't know how Venedians react to children. She's taking care of her, but only when I'm not around.

It just proves that we're perfect partners.

Chapter Fourteen

Kisho

Being locked up in a small space was the last place Kisho wanted to be, but there he was, all over again. This time he was locked in with a woman and a small baby. As much as he'd like to freak out over the cramped space and lack of any real light, Dido was already doing that enough for the three of them and if he joined in they'd probably suffocate. He'd taken the child from her when he realized she was more afraid than he was and just started rambling.

"Well hello there little thing, you don't know it, but you are being held by the most amazing man in the entire galaxy. Did you know, that my sexual prowess is renowned on multiple planets? That somewhere there is a statue of me and unsatisfied women pray to it hoping that I will once again visit their primitive planet. Of course you don't know that because you're a baby and that would be ridiculous, but one day that will impress you.

"In fact, I guarantee that it will impress you unless you are like your auntie Jutel who is an enigma of a woman. Did you know, that she didn't want her sole purpose in life to be satisfying me? I didn't word it exactly like that, I'm not an idiot mind you, but I did give her the option to live that way for the last couple of weeks. Believe it or not she turned me down. In all my years, which they aren't that many I assure you, I've never been turned down by a woman.

"Maybe I'm losing my charm. What do you think?"

He paused and looked down at the child and was rewarded with a huge toothless grin.

"I didn't think so. I'll have to think of another way to woo the beautiful Jutel because I don't know how long I can take being on her bad side. Though, her frowns are adorable, I'm less amused by the lack of pleasure. Your uncle Kisho has never gone this long without a woman or man, I was not meant for this kind of isolation."

Dido, who had calmed down while he talked, said, "Do you really think that's appropriate conversation for a baby?"

"She has no idea what I'm saying, so I don't see the problem, plus I'm hoping she'll give me some good advice. Jutel loves her, if I can figure out how to duplicate whatever it is she's doing maybe I could successfully gain Jutel's affection. Also, you really need to come up with a name for this child, she's a month old she needs something better than a pronoun."

Silence descended between the three of them and Kisho started to feel the walls closing in. Before he could lose his cool, though, Dido said, "I'm afraid to name her. What if someone takes her? If I name her won't I feel worse if that happens?"

"I doubt it. How could you feel worse whether

she's got a name or not? You're still going to want her back, you're still going to wish she was with you. Having a name doesn't make that any less. You're being silly, not that your fears aren't justified, but not naming her because she might be taken just causes confusion when people are talking about her."

Kisho wasn't known for his sensitivity but he felt like he'd handled that admirably.

"Natsuki, her name is Natsuki."

"That's a beautiful name, I actually had a great aunt named Natsuki. She was a surprisingly lovely woman among a sea of self-satisfying pompous pricks. Good choice."

Dido's mouth quirked up but she didn't say anything so he continued to ramble. He lost track of how long they were locked away, at some point Dido and Natsuki fell asleep, which didn't work out well for him because he didn't have anyone to distract him from his fear. He continued talking, but with no one to respond he wasn't as distracted as before.

Hours passed and finally he felt the ship move. They must be taking off. Soon surely, they would be let out of their hiding spot. They couldn't keep them here forever, right? He'd just leave, he could do that, right? Unless they'd locked them in, they wouldn't do that, would they? He could just see Jutel doing that to him all because he'd wanted to have sex with her.

The door opened and the woman he was thinking about stood in front of him. She offered him a hand but instead of taking it he said, "You're a beautiful woman, of course I want to have sex with you. I'm getting tired of being in the dog house just because I suggested it. You need to get over whatever you were offended by because you know damn well I wasn't meaning to be offensive."

He shoved Natsuki into her arms and pulled himself out of the hole and stomped down the hallway to his cabin. He needed a bath, but a shower was just going to have to do. Halfway down the corridor he noticed the door to an unused cabin was open. Curious he popped his head in and was shocked to see someone new.

"Who are you?

The well-built muscular man looked up at Kisho and grinned. He jumped up from the computer he'd been setting up and said, "I'm Raiden, I joined you on the last stop."

"No shit. Who are you? Why are you here?"

Raiden looked a little startled but Kisho was too busy taking in his competition to notice that he was being rude, not that that would change anything.

"Um, my parents are friends with Jutel and they asked her to keep me out of trouble. So here I am."

Kisho frowned at him before comprehension dawned. Smiling he said, "Oh, I see how it is. You're one of those alien races that bulk up early, right? You're like a man-child. Perfect. Stick with me and you'll see all the trouble you want."

Raiden gave him a confused smile before Kisho left the room and headed to his own. He'd been concerned there for a minute, not that he should have been. No one was competition for him and this adolescent wouldn't get between him and Jutel. No she was all woman and needed a man for her needs and that's where Kisho fit.

Mal's Notes

We've got another new crew member, I wonder if Raiden is going to create a love triangle? I hope not, I've never been fond of those. I know Jutel doesn't think she likes Kisho but I've never seen someone spend so much time covertly watching someone they're supposed to be ignoring. It's hilarious.

God I'm pathetic, living vicariously through my friends like this. I seriously need to get off this ship. At the very least the next person we pick up better be a female.

I think I'll mess with Bill some, keep him on his toes. He's younger than me after all, if anyone should have gotten Dido it should have been me. Not that I'm attracted to her, but he doesn't know that, and it could be entertaining to see how he reacts.

Chapter Fifteen

Jutel

Well that had been unexpected. Anika had led Jutel to believe that Raiden was a boy, maybe a teenager, but he was clearly a man. He'd actually laughed when she first saw him because her mouth might have dropped open.

Maybe.

Yeah it had.

"She forgets I'm not a baby anymore, the only thing that saves me from constant parental intervention are my six other siblings, even then they love to use me as a diversion when they're getting in trouble. Now they're on their own though.

"Thanks for agreeing to take me, I've been dying to get out there in the universe but dad was blocking me. He kept saying to just give him time and he'd find someone he trusted to take me out. I didn't know he'd find someone so beautiful to do it though."

He winked at her and for some unexplainable reason she blushed. She actually blushed. She never blushed, she just—didn't. He chuckled and then led the way up the ramp of The Flower. She stood there for a minute and wondered what she was going to do. Thank goodness for Dido, at least she wasn't the only woman on board.

She went to the cockpit and then realized she didn't know where to go. She didn't want to head toward Vende even though that's what Kisho wanted, but she couldn't think of another alternative. She needed to talk to the crew, but she had to get off the planet first. Sighing she set the autopilot for Vende with every intention of changing the heading as soon as possible.

The ship received clearance and took off, clearing the atmosphere with no problems. Once they jumped into hyperspace Jutel went to let Kisho and Dido out of the hidden cubby. When she'd commissioned that part of the ship she'd never expected to use it this frequently, if ever. It had just been something she thought would give the ship some added character, like having a secret passage in your home. Now she'd used it twice and she still wasn't sure if she'd done the right thing.

Opening the door she offered Kisho her hand.

"You're a beautiful woman, of course I want to have sex with you. I'm getting tired of being in the dog house just because I suggested it. You need to get over whatever you were offended by because you know damn well I wasn't meaning to be offensive."

Eyes wide she looked over his shoulder at Dido who appeared as though she'd been sleeping. He shoved the baby in Jutel's arms then pushed past her. Looking over her shoulder she saw him stop at Raiden's door and she couldn't stop her groan. She'd been hoping to forestall any meeting they had because she knew it was going to be bad. Kisho had a very high opinion of himself and if another male appeared that threatened that she had no idea what he'd do.

Looking down at the baby in her arms she didn't know if she should follow him or just ignore it and hope whatever happened blew over. She could hear the beginnings of Kisho and Raiden's exchange but Dido's hand on her arm as she pried herself from the cramped quarters brought her attention back to what she'd been doing.

"I'm sorry you were in there so long. I hope that Kisho didn't drive you crazy."

Dido smiled and took the baby, "No, he was fine. I'm not fond of tight spaces and he kept me and Natsuki distracted so I didn't lose it."

"Natsuki?"

"Yes, Kisho pointed out that I had neglected to name my daughter and that is the name I chose."

"It's beautiful."

Dido nodded her head, beaming down at her child, "Yes it is, thank you. We're going to my room now."

She was halfway to her cabin when Jutel remembered all that she needed to ask. "Dido, I'm sorry, I'm sure you're tired, but I need to speak with you and the rest of the crew immediately. Could you please go to the galley?"

Hesitating Dido had a sudden look of fear on her face before it was replaced with a blank expression. She dipped her head, but didn't respond, instead she changed her course and Jutel watched as she disappeared toward the ships kitchen and dining area.

Knocking on Mal then Bill's door she asked them to meet her there as well. She paused before knocking on the side of Raiden's door, he hadn't closed it. He was technically part of the crew but she didn't know if he would add anything to the discussion. Shrugging her shoulders she decided he should at least be there to listen. "Raiden we're having a crew meeting in the galley if you could head up there, it shouldn't take too long then you can come back and get your room situated."

He looked up from equipment he'd been tinkering with on the floor and grinned at her. She could feel the blush rising again and wished desperately that it would stop doing that. He was barely legal, he shouldn't have that power over her. He stood up and grabbed a large painting that was leaning against the wall. She hadn't noticed it until now and the way it was laying she had no idea what it was. When he turned it around she saw the painting she'd lusted after.

"My mother knows how much you love this piece. As a thank you for taking me in she wanted me to give it to you."

He offered it to her and she felt a lump in her throat as she took it. Swallowing past it she smiled and said, "Thank you. I kept meaning to ask her about it, but I never got around to it. Not that I could have afforded it. She didn't have to."

"She wanted too."

Nodding her head she could feel her blush deepening. Ignoring it, she quickly dropped the painting off in her room and made her way to Kisho's closed door.

He opened the door naked, his cock semi erect, his hair tousled. Regular meals were really working for him. No longer did he appear sickly and underweight. He would never have the bulk of Raiden, but his slender build had some advantages.

"We're having a crew meeting in the galley."

"When?"

"Right now."

He leaned against the door and put on what she'd learned he thought was a charming smile and said, "Are you sure we can't postpone it, for just a little while?"

His cock jumped at his words but she refused to take the bait and look. Her body, betrayed her, though, and she felt her nipples pebble at his words. Thank goodness her clothes hid that. Why did Kisho illicit that kind of response, while Raiden could cause her to blush? It didn't make sense.

Confused at the way her body reacted to the two men and angry at them both because of it, she glared at Kisho and said, "Be there in five minutes or you won't get any say in our future plans."

Turing on her heel she left the crew quarters and somehow managed not to stomp to the galley where most of them were already waiting. On the threshold she took a calming breath, and then decided to get a cup of coffee before joining the others at the table. By the time she was finished they were all waiting for her.

"For everyone that doesn't already know, we picked up a new crew member on Andove." She did a quick series of introductions before continuing. "We need to figure out what our next move is. Right now we have no cargo and no jobs. We've got enough money to cover rations for the next couple of months so we don't need to rush, but I don't want to wait around."

"We need to head to Vende, I have business there, and as soon as it's concluded you'll never have to work again. I'll see to that."

Kisho winked at Jutel and she stared blankly at him before he dropped his eyes and grumbled under his breath, something that she didn't even bother trying to hear. Turning to Dido, who had gone still at the mention of Vende, Jutel softened her tone and asked, "Dido, do you have something you want to add?"

Jutel hoped the woman would speak up, tell them what Jutel already knew, but she just shook her head violently, clutching Natsuki close to her chest. Sighing Jutel looked around the table before beginning. "The UUAC is searching for an escaped 'servant' of His Majesty the Emperor of Vende. She went missing on Benjo and the emperor is very insistent she be returned immediately. That was why we had such a warm greeting on Andove."

Her voice a bit firmer this time she turned back to Dido and asked again, "Do you have something you want to add Dido?"

The woman wouldn't meet her gaze and Jutel felt bad about forcing her to answer, but they needed to make a decision and without her input they could find themselves in an even worse situation.

Finally Dido said, "I'm not a servant. Servants get paid, servants have a choice. I was his slave, his forced concubine, his favorite until I bore him a daughter, but as soon as I get rid of Natsuki he'll take me back, he assured me."

She looked disgusted at the words and Jutel couldn't blame her. She wanted to comfort the woman, but didn't think now was the time. She shot Mal a glance and he scooted closer to the woman but didn't touch her. Bill glared at them both before scooting closer on her other side. Well that was interesting, but now was not the time to think about it.

"I think, it's in our best interest, if we go someplace other than Vende."

"What?! We have to, I *need* to get to Vende as soon as possible."

Her eyes went to Kisho and she waited for him to calm down before she said, "The last place we need to take Dido right now is the planet that she's escaped from. We should be taking her somewhere safe, like Nian."

Kisho snorted at that, "You think Nian would be safe from the emperor? That will be the first place he looks. Do you trust your government to keep an escaped slave hidden?"

There was a sharp intake of breath from Dido at his words and everyone at the table glared at him but Jutel felt a sinking feeling in the pit of her stomach. The Nian government didn't like to interfere and if the emperor or anyone from Vende showed up claiming Dido had done something illegal then they would hand her over. At best Jutel could promise her safety for a limited time. There had to be another option though.

"What better place to hide her than the last place they'd look? Who in their right mind would expect Dido to go back to Vende? That would be the last place they'd look."

Using twisted logic Jutel could see where he was coming from, but going to Vende was still too dangerous. Turning to Dido she asked, "What do you want to do? Kisho is right, I can't guarantee your safety on Nian, however Nian isn't the only planet out there. We could try someplace else."

Dido looked at her in confusion and Jutel realized this was probably the first time anyone had ever asked her what she wanted. Everyone around the table waited silently, even Kisho who very clearly wanted to try and sway the woman to his side of things. Dido's eyes dropped and she whispered, "I want to go home. I want to see my family, show them Natsuki."

Jutel gave the woman a small smile but inside she felt defeated. Going to Vende was not a good idea, but she'd given the option to Dido and she didn't want to snatch it away. Did she exert authoritative control, proclaim herself the captain and thus the leader of this bunch of crazies, or did she do what they wanted?

Sighing she stood up and said, "I'll think about it. For now, we're on our way to Vende. Unless I change my mind it will take four weeks to get there. I'll be in my cabin if anyone wants to discuss our options."

She hated being in charge, but being democratic didn't seem like a good option either.

Bill's Journal

Mal better not think for one minute he can try and take my woman. I don't care how nice he's been to me, Dido is mine.

Stupid visions, if they were working I would know what to do, how to keep her at my side. Going to Vende doesn't seem right, but if Dido wants it I'll stand behind her. It would be so much easier to keep her safe if I could see the future.

Even though I want to keep her safe, there's a part of me that loves this new freedom.

Chapter Sixteen

Kisho

Excellent, everything was working out. Though, Jutel wasn't happy about that, he knew she'd get over it. It's not like going to Vende was a horrible idea. The minute Kisho arrived he'd head to the head magistrate's office and start private negotiations to pay for his silence. If the price was right he could easily forget that he was the rightful emperor. Who wanted that job anyway?

A week had passed since Jutel's little meeting and so far they were still on course. Dido had been unconvinced by Mal's pleas to change her mind, which made Kisho's job even easier. He just left the fighting to her and sat back and watched. Things were certainly more pleasurable this time around, though, Jutel was still angry with him and hadn't come back to his bed. She wasn't in Raiden's bed either, which was good.

Raiden had been a curve ball. At first Kisho hadn't felt threatened, the man-child had nothing on Kisho's sexual prowess and even if Jutel spent a night in his bed it would only be one. However, she hadn't spent a night in Raiden's bed and instead blushed whenever he was around. It was insulting. He was barely more than a child and not worth the attention of a woman like Jutel, but Kisho had decided to play the long game. He sat back and watched, even though he was seething inside. He tried not to let her actions affect him.

In three short weeks none of it would matter anyway. He would be on Vende and incredibly wealthy shortly after that. He would have access to the most beautiful and talented women across the universe and he could forget Jutel.

For now, though, that was going to be difficult. The woman was everywhere on the ship, the only way to escape her was to stay in his room and that wasn't going to happen. Kisho needed stimulation or he would go stir crazy.

"This is all your fault."

The beautiful seething voice of the woman haunting his dreams met his ears and he realized she'd snuck up on him. He'd been in the cargo bay looking down as Mal and Bill completed a holo-sim of some novel written by an earthling that lived on Nian.

"What's my fault? I haven't done anything, though if it gets you to talk to me I'd do whatever I didn't do all over again."

Jutel stared at him blankly before rolling her eyes and huffing. "You know exactly what I'm talking about. You put this stupid idea in Dido's head and she won't let it go. The worst place in this universe for her is Vende and you know it."

"I know no such thing. I can think of a handful of planets ten times worse than Vende for Dido to go to."

"You are purposefully being obtuse. Talk to

her, tell her that she shouldn't go. We've all tried at this point, even Raiden, but none of us can get her to change her mind. She wants to see her family. We can take her someplace safe, then go get her family, but she refuses. She says that they won't come, that she has to go to them. This is ridiculous!"

Why did she have to bring up Raiden? Why had she even talked to him? He wasn't a part of this. He shouldn't have an opinion one way or the other. It rankled him. Kisho turned away from her and leaned on the railing overlooking the bay. His hands crossed in front of him and he clenched his teeth to keep from responding. It didn't work, and he ended up being harsher than he probably should have been.

"You aren't mad at me, you're mad at yourself. You've put yourself in a position of authority on this ship and you hate it, but you hate the idea of giving that control to anyone else even more. In some twisted last ditch effort to not take control, you've given all the authority to a one time slave that probably hasn't even had any kind of higher education, so she's making her choice based on emotion. If you were really a captain, you wouldn't ask anyone what to do you'd fucking do it. You'd weigh the pros and cons, make your decision and act. Instead, you're sitting there like your damn hands are tied when they aren't.

"So grow a spine, take control, and stop fucking blaming me for your situation."

He didn't turn around but he could almost hear her grinding her teeth. He gave her a minute before looking over his shoulder and she was gone. Sighing, his head dropped and he wondered why he had to be so attracted to stubborn women. There ought to be a support group.

Raiden's Log

I'm not normally one for writing stuff down like this, but everyone on this odd ship seems to be doing it. Well Mal and Bill at least. Those two are kind of weird. So are Kisho and Jutel for that matter. I wonder if they know that Dido is lying. Should I mention it to someone? I'm not even sure what she's lying about. Maybe if I hack into Vende's systems I can discover more about her.

I'll do that, then talk to Jutel. The more information I have the better.

Chapter Seventeen

Jutel

Pacing in her cabin Jutel fumed. "How dare he, stupid fucking man, he has no idea—I am not giving—I *can* give up control anytime I damn well please."

She could barely finish a thought after speaking with Kisho. The man was infuriating on a level never before achieved by a living being. He could win awards. He was so—the word was just out of reach and she was mortified when it came into focus. He was right.

Eyes wide she sat down heavily on the chair in her room. Bringing her feet up she pulled the blanket from the back of it around her and tried to draw comfort from the cushy furniture. She wasn't weak, but that didn't mean she wanted power, especially power over the lives of the people she cared for. Mal, Bill, and even the new people meant too much for her to be in control. What if she screwed up again? What if she decided she knew the right course, put them on it, and discovered she was wrong?

Closing her eyes she rested her head on her knees and tried to figure out what to do. They had no job, there were none available on the job boards. They at least had enough credits for food for a while. She had a thief on board who drove her crazy and needed to get to Vende for reasons she was too afraid to ask about. She had an escaped slave who happened to have been owned by the reigning emperor of Vende, a man that was apparently very keen on getting her back. She also happened to have the daughter of that emperor on board and who knew where she stood in the line of succession, if at all.

The only two people on board not causing conflict were Mal and Bill. Well, there was Raiden and he wasn't really doing anything either. He spent all his time on his computers only occasionally leaving his room to use the holo-suite to run an exercise routine and for whatever reason he only ever did that when she was there. Watching him exercise put her in a perpetual state of blushing, it was ridiculous. She really enjoyed looking at his body, but his cocky glances and winks didn't do anything to her, they didn't make her think about plastering him to the floor and riding him to oblivion, for some reason her body was only reacting that way to Kisho.

She forced her mind away from that train of thought. She had no desire to go there again. She'd slept with him, it had been very satisfying, memorable even, but she couldn't do it again. She needed to focus on what to do and not about the annoying passengers on board the ship or how they made her feel and the ideas they put in her mind.

Bill and Mal were being annoying lately too. Both men seemed to have set their sights on Dido, who appeared to be completely oblivious to it. They were always at her cabin bringing her food and water and taking care of the child. Seriously, Natsuki was the only member of the crew that wasn't giving Jutel a headache.

Standing up again Jutel returned to pacing, forcing her mind on the issue. She had two choices. She could continue the course and got to Vende. That's what Kisho wanted and it's what Dido wanted. Or she could go—someplace else? Nian was her first choice, but she didn't know if they'd accept Dido there. Vende was a powerful planet and could potentially attack Nian and take her by force if the emperor so decided. Nian defenses were strong, but they'd been untested for a very long time.

The question boiled down to how much the emperor of Vende wanted Dido. If he was willing to attack Nian or even just go to Nian with false charges, then she really shouldn't take Dido to Vende. Of course, then she had to figure out where to take her. Did he really want her that bad, though? Sure he'd sent someone to Andove, but that didn't mean anything, did it?

Dido was just one woman, one child, were they really worth the effort she was assuming he would go to?

Shaking her head, Jutel tried to look at it logically. It had taken the emperor nothing to have one of his captains ask about the possibility she was on board ship. Dido, didn't seem to think there was any risk in going back to Vende. So far, there wasn't anything that pointed to the emperor going to great extremes to get Dido or the child. So why did she think they shouldn't go to Vende?

Gut instinct.

Groaning Jutel shook her head. Gut instinct wasn't a reason she could go to her crew and use.

They'd want something more tangible than that, at least Dido and Kisho would. Why had she picked up new people?

Oh yeah, she hadn't been given a choice. Bill had brought Dido and Kisho had just stowed away. Why had the universe done this to her?

"Fine, whatever, they want to go to Vende we'll fucking go to Vende. I don't have a better option and I have no reason to think that anything will happen if we do. I mean, it's not like Captain Fah even pushed the issue. He didn't even manually search The Flower."

Her decision made, Jutel expected to feel relieved, but if anything she felt even more anxious. Leaving her room she went to the galley and found everyone already there for the evening meal. They all stopped what they were doing and looked to her, waiting, it was like they knew she'd finally come to a conclusion.

"We're going to Vende."

Dido and Kisho looked relieved, happy even. The rest of the crew, not so much, but none of them questioned her or forced the issue. Not hungry Jutel left the galley and headed back to her room. Maybe if she got some sleep she'd feel better about everything.

Mal's Notes

I've made no progress on my story. You'd think with all the tension on this ship I'd be inspired, but nope. The words aren't coming at all.

I'm going stir crazy.

I've watched and re-watched my favorite soaps. I've teased Bill to the point where I'm beginning to wonder if I should sleep with one eye open. Kisho isn't providing any entertainment and Raiden spends all of his time sitting at a computer, it's a wonder the man looks like a body builder.

Space flight sucks.

Chapter Eighteen

Kisho

Kisho couldn't keep the grin from his face even when he tried. With every passing day they got closer and closer to Vende, which meant they were closer and closer to him being wealthy again.

He'd been raised with wealth, he'd never had to work, he'd had the best of everything, and then all that had changed.

His father had been killed. Kisho should have been crowned the new emperor, but then someone had tried to kill him too. He'd escaped, barely, but in all the chaos that had ensued afterwards, he'd been declared dead and his two bit cousin had been declared the emperor. It should have been easy for him to show up and declare to the world that he was alive, but things were rarely easy when it came to ruling one of the wealthiest planets in the universe.

That's why he'd stolen the bio-reader. He now had definitive proof, that couldn't be tampered with, that he was the rightful heir. There was even a whole group of people on Vende that thought he was still alive and that the rightful emperor wasn't on the throne.

Well, he didn't want the throne, he wanted a fortune. He'd never wanted to rule, way too much work for his taste, but the little bit of money he'd been able to get his hands on before his accounts had been cleared by the royal treasury had been spent a lot faster than it should have been. Broke and starving he'd scraped by planning for over a year what he needed to do.

Now, here he was, the finish line and fabulous wealth almost in his grasp. All he had to do was make it to Vende.

He tried not to let Jutel's moping affect him and focused instead on that goal. Why did she have to do it in front of him, though? Everywhere he turned she was there looking like she'd just made the worst decision of her life. It's not like he was even the reason she'd made the decision, he wasn't an idiot. His desire had never come into play in her choice, it had been all about Dido. So why did he feel bad about it?

"Infernal woman."

He'd never really thought about how small The Flower was until he started trying to avoid Jutel and found that he couldn't. Why did it even matter? She wasn't his in any sense of the word. She didn't even like him, so why did her feelings matter? She was just some Nian warrior woman that had shot him multiple times, locked him in a small space, and grudgingly ferried him around the universe. Never mind that she didn't have to do any of that and could have just dumped him out the airlock and no one would have cared.

Why did she have to be so damn—nice? He didn't even like nice. He liked bad women. Women that wanted to do things that were illegal on less enlightened planets. He'd had sex with Jutel already, his appetite for her should be wetted, instead he kept himself up at night thinking up ways to get back in her bed. His small taste had been like a god damn drug that was going to be in his system forever.

It was starting to mess with his mind. He couldn't enjoy the sonic shower or even take matters into his own hands. He was starting to think of ways to get back on her good side, ways that didn't involve sex. He'd become a shell of himself all for a woman that despised his very existence.

Maybe that was the problem. Jutel wasn't the first woman to rebuff his advances, but she was the first that Kisho actually wanted. He was attracted to her, she was sexy and self-reliant and something about the fact that she could kick his ass really turned him on. He was clearly suffering from some kind of space sickness. It had to be about availability to women, he'd felt something similar before. If you've got limited access then you're naturally attracted to whatever's available. Right? Yes. That had to be it.

They couldn't get to Vende fast enough.

Bill's Journal

Dido seems to change before my eyes the closer we get to Vende. At first I thought she was afraid to return, but when I asked her she said I was being silly. The more I study her the more I realize that she's excited to return. I don't understand.

I've been traveling the galaxy for half a decade and not once have I returned to Olovia. I've thought about it and I don't necessarily fear returning to the planet that enslaved me and my people, but I certainly don't get excited at the prospect.

While I was rocking Natsuki to sleep last night I started to wonder if maybe Dido was suffering from Stockholm syndrome. I'm not even sure if it's a real mental disease, but the people on Mal's programs seem to suffer from it occasionally, they're always getting kidnapped then falling in love with their captors.

All I can think to do is be there for her when we land. Make sure that she understands that she and Natsuki have options.

Chapter Nineteen

Jutel

She'd lost weight. The closer they got to Vende the more worried she grew and the less she ate. Not one to keep on excess weight, even less than normal since lately food wasn't always plentiful, Jutel was starting to look gaunt. They were minutes from landing and all she could think was something was terribly wrong.

Standing in front of Bill's door she hesitated for a moment before ringing the bell. The door slid open and Bill looked at her in surprise. "Is everything alright?"

"Can I come in?"

"Sure." He backed up and she followed him, keying the door closed. He looked at her curiously but didn't say anything while she shifted nervously in front of him.

She eyed him with concern before saying, "Have you seen anything? I know that you said you were having issues, but I feel deep in my bones that something is wrong and I don't know why. I'd feel better if you could tell me you'd seen something."

He gave her an apologetic smile and said, "I haven't seen anything at all in weeks. Not even the little bits and pieces I was seeing before, it's like I'm being blocked by something. It's never happened before, ever. It's—amazing. I'm sorry, I should have said something earlier but I've been enjoying the freedom of not knowing. My entire life I haven't had that before."

She felt even worse now, what could possibly be blocking Bill's powerful gift? They were minutes from approaching hailing distance and getting their docking clearance and she had no clue what was going to happen. The only positive was that Dido and Kisho had needed to land in the same place, the capital city.

"Just—let me know if anything changes."

"Of course, Jutel. I'm sure it doesn't mean everything, it's all going to be alright."

She nodded absently as she left his room and headed to the cockpit. Kisho was already there waiting but he didn't say anything to her. They'd reached a kind of peace in the last week. She wasn't jumping into his bed, but she'd stopped being angry at him. He'd been right and it was stupid to be mad at someone because of that. Knowing Kisho, though, it was only a matter of time before he said something to make her angry again.

They sat in silence and surprisingly Jutel felt comforted by it.

"I can't wait to get off this ship. I swear if I didn't already have an appointment set up I'd find the nearest brothel and decimate their ranks."

Well that had lasted longer than expected.

"I'm glad to see that your time with us hasn't changed you Kisho."

He gave her his best charming smile and despite herself she returned it. She would never admit it out loud, but she was going to miss him. It was ridiculous, he was annoying and said some of the most offensive things, but after four weeks he'd grown on her. She knew that half the time he wasn't as serious as he'd want you to believe and while she knew that he really did think he was god's gift to women it wasn't too annoying. At least not all the time. Plus he was pretty good in that department.

Turning away from him before she said something that led to another lewd comment she looked at the ships controls. They were in range. Taking a deep breath she sent the standard docking request and waited.

"You're too nervous, nothing is going to go wrong. Vende has less crime than almost any other planet in the universe. You've got nothing to worry about."

"Yeah, and slavery is supposed to be illegal in the UUAC, but then you've got Dido."

He frowned but didn't respond which made her sad. She was hoping that he'd come up with something that she'd missed, at the very least take her mind off of things.

The ship dinged letting her know their docking request had been approved and the ship's autopilot locked onto their assigned location with ease. Vende had a high amount of air and space traffic, but they were so old that they had it worked out to a science and everything moved quickly and efficiently.

The ship landed smoothly and that was it, after four weeks and an almost constant state of anxiety, they were on Vende. Now it was time to see if all of her worry was for nothing.

Raiden's Log

Well, I wasn't able to hack into the Vende systems, their security is better than anything I've ever seen, excluding Nian security. I actually had to ask Mal for access to The Flower's computers, something I've never had to do in my entire life. If people back home find out my reputation will be ruined.

Anyway, I may not have been able to hack into the Vende network, but I was able to hack into the UUAC's. I learned a lot about Jutel and Mal in there, if even half the shit they did while trying to win the UUAC's favor is true they're incredible. I seriously can't believe they let themselves get strung along for so long. Did they not realize the UUAC was using them? That they were expected to fail and end up dead?

I guess not. At least now I know why they're both so temperamental and depressing. If I'd seen what they had, I don't know—

Chapter Twenty

Kisho

Four weeks and no sex later Kisho was home. Stepping off the ramp of The Flower he nearly bounced in excitement. He slapped Mal and Raiden on the back, avoided Bill though he hadn't been too annoying lately, and he told Dido to look him up. Then he pulled Jutel into his arms, dipped her low, and gave her a kiss she'd never forget.

When he lifted her back up he was rewarded with glassy eyes and a flushed face. He was also pretty sure she'd let him do that and the fact that she'd kissed him back didn't bode well for him getting over her fast. The only thing to do was to get his money and find a bordello fast.

"I'll see ya'll around, look me up if you're ever back on Vende, though, who knows how long I'll be here."

He waved goodbye and that was that. He didn't like to drag things out. They'd let him know they were going to rejoin Dido with her family, but he hadn't shared his plans with them.

He looked back once. Just once, and he was pleased to see that Jutel was looking after him. He still had it.

Swaggering through the capital city he kept waiting for someone to recognize him, but it didn't happen. He started looking around taking in everything that had changed and not changed. They'd been given clearance to dock at a surprisingly upscale part of town, normally those berths were for more elite visitors, but maybe they'd been given the space because they had a Nian ship. Nians still had a name throughout the galaxy, though most people were starting to forget that name.

Shrugging his shoulders he wasted no time thinking about the docking habits of the Vende port captain and instead started going over what he was going to buy first with his new fortune.

His hair was a mess, his nails horrific, and his muscles were so tense. Before anything he was going to get all that taken care of, then he would tackle his severely lacking wardrobe. Once he had the basics he would visit his favorite club, the one with the naked dancers and never ending booze. God he missed the days of his misspent youth.

Glancing down at his comm he realized he'd been wasting time. His appointment with the magistrate's office was coming up and the last thing he needed to be was late. He'd never met the magistrate, he wasn't someone that Kisho would have met in his position, but now he was the only one that could get his offer to the emperor.

Walking at a very brisk pace, since running was not approved unless there was an emergency and absolutely necessary, Kisho arrived just in time.

There was a line. Apparently he was not going to be speaking to the head magistrate, but had to first make his way up through the ranks. Things weren't looking good.

Half an hour later when he was finally able to speak with someone he said, "I had an appointment half an hour ago, can I just go back?"

The woman behind the desk looked at him like he was a moron and just grabbed his thumb and pressed it to the pad before screaming out, "Next!"

The screen behind her popped up a number and he was told to follow the arrows to a waiting room, when his number was called *then* he could go back. He was in hell.

The waiting room was crowded and smelled funny. There were old people and clearly homeless people, and the lowest of the low in society everywhere. The seats were uncomfortable and all the available entertainment was taken. Every few minutes a person looking just as put out as the receptionist from earlier would appear from behind a closed door and call a number. The prisoner, because that's what Kisho was beginning to think they were, would rush up and they'd disappear down a long hallway before the door would slam shut behind them. No one should be treated this way, especially on Vende.

Three hours passed and Kisho flip flopped between anger and nerves. He just wanted to get this over and done with so he could return to his rightful life. Closing in on the fourth hour a well-dressed man opened the door. He scanned the faces in the room, before coming to a stop on Kisho's. Sitting up straight he returned the man's stare, waiting for him to call his number. Instead four officers of the Vende military marched in, surrounding him.

"What's going on here? I'm a Venedian citizen, I've been waiting for four hours to see someone about an urgent matter. What are these soldiers doing?"

No one spoke to him. The room grew eerily silent as his fellow detainees moved as far away from him as they could get. Someone behind Kisho grabbed his elbow and pulled him to a standing position, they then marched him down the hallway and he heard the door slam shut behind him.

Mal's Notes

Hopefully Vende gives me some inspiration. These last four weeks have been hellish. Surrounded by Jutel and Kisho mooning at each other but neither acting was boring. Then there's Bill who looks at Dido like he's never seen a woman before. She, on the other hand, only notices him when Natsuki needs to be fed or changed. It's kind of pathetic and definitely not something I want to write about.

Where's the love and adventure? Why can't life be like a soap opera?

Chapter Twenty-One

Jutel

"So Dido, where exactly are your family? Did you want to call them to meet you somewhere or did you want to try them at their home? Do they have a home?" Bill's voice sounded almost manic when he spoke.

He was not his usual self and Jutel missed that. He seemed uncertain and despite what he'd told her it looked like the lack of psychic ability was starting to get to him. Dido gave him a small smile before her eyes dropped and she held Natsuki tighter.

"I think it would be best to see them at home. It's not far, I promise. In fact you don't need to go with me."

Jutel's eyes darted to Dido's face but didn't see anything amiss, however, her tone seemed off. Something wasn't right but Jutel still didn't know what. Putting a big smile on her face she placed her hand on Dido's shoulder and squeezed, maybe a bit too tight, and said, "Don't be silly. We've come with you this far, we're all looking forward to a family reunion."

Dido didn't respond instead she started walking

away. Bill and Mal exchanged a look before glancing at Jutel. They all turned and fell in step behind Dido. They walked through the busy city, easily keeping up with her even though she walked fast. Not once did she look around her or try and avoid the gaze of policemen and other authority figures.

Forty five minutes later they were on the front doorstep of a huge building. At first glance it seemed to be a giant apartment building, at least that's what Jutel thought. But when Dido pressed an intercom button Jutel realized it was just one home. Did Dido's family work here?

A face appeared on the intercom for barely a second before a gasp of surprise came over the comm. Light from a scanner covered Dido's face as it verified her identity. It took less than a minute before the light flashed green and the door was flung open. A Venedian dressed in a very formal uniform appeared. He gave Dido a deep bow and she transformed before their eyes. She lost the air of a woman beaten down by the world. Her back straightened, her chin tilted up and her eyes grew hard.

She shoved Natsuki into the man's arms and said, "Cleves please take care of this. I'll see mother in the blue parlor immediately. As soon as that's over, I'd like to take a long hot bath and have the clothes I'm wearing burned. Once that's done we'll need to contact the domestic minister, let him know there's a new Imperial Princess and the line of succession is being changed, unless we can come to an agreement."

"Dido?" Bill's voice sounded confused and his hand rose as if he was going to reach out to her. She looked at him over her shoulder and his hand hovered in the air before dropping to his side. Her eyes were cold, gone was the woman they had felt a need to protect and shelter, in her place was someone they'd never met before.

Her eyes rested on each of them for barely a second each before she turned back and took a step over the threshold, the last thing they heard her say was, "Cleves see to these people. Give them some money or something. Not much of course, but they did make sure I arrived in one piece and kept me out of the hands of our grasping, incompetent emperor."

She disappeared into the house and they quickly lost sight of her. Bill and Mal were both in a daze. Jutel was—shocked of course, a little betrayed, but most of all relieved. If that was the worst that happened on Vende then she'd walk away happy.

Cleves looked down his nose as though waiting for them to beg or grovel. His eyes met Jutel's and she cocked her hip to the side and said, "So how about that money?"

His lip curled in distaste but he moved Natsuki from one arm to the other before pulling out a personal comm unit. He fiddled with it then held it out for Jutel to place her thumb to. No words were exchanged and the only noise that was made was a slight gurgle from Natsuki. That actually caused Jutel to feel a pang of regret. The little girl had been adorable, the ship was going to be lonely without her.

As soon as the screen flashed green signaling the completion of the money transfer Cleves stepped back and firmly closed the door in their faces. The three friends slowly walked back to the street away from the house. Mal had a half smile on his lips and appeared to have recovered from the shock. Jutel was concerned about Bill, though, for the first time in all the years she'd known him he looked angry.

"I can't believe she lied to me, to all of us. We helped her, I saved her from—she lied to us!" He was positively vibrating with fury and Jutel grew worried thinking about what he might do.

Mal must have felt the same because he threw his arm of Bill's shoulder and said, "We're docked at one of the most famous cities in the galaxy, we were just paid what I'm hoping is a sizeable sum, and we don't have anywhere to be. Why don't you and I go get drunk and marvel at how cruel the universe can be? Jutel, you aren't invited, I'm afraid you're the enemy tonight."

Mal grinned at her but Bill just shook out of Mal's hold and walked away. Mal rushed after him shouting to Jutel that he'd keep them out of any serious trouble. She frowned as the two disappeared and wondered if she should follow.

The Vende capital was known for its low crime rate and friendliness to visitors, plus Bill would never do anything too foolish, he was too level headed. More than likely he just needed some time to get over his hurt feelings and he'd move on. He'd never been in love before so this was a harsh lesson to learn.

Tugging her ear lobe out of habit Jutel walked down the street toward the center of the city. Data streamed across her retina and she read it with interest. Vende's capital city was called Life, the Venedians believed it was where life on the planet began, and in the center of the town was a massive tree and a river that parted around it. Some guidebooks listed it as one of the wonders of the galaxy. Maybe, if she were lucky, she'd get to see it. Maybe the beauty and nature would give her guidance about what to do next.

"So where too?"

Startled Jutel looked up and realized that Raiden was following her. The blush, which was never too far from her when he was around, stained her cheeks when she realized that she hadn't even noticed that he had followed them from the ship.

"Sorry I didn't see you there."

He grinned at her and shoved his hands in his pockets before saying, "I know, it's okay, you guys were distracted. People forget I'm here all the time."

She gave an unladylike snort and rolled her eyes, "I doubt that."

His grin grew and it was like something clicked inside of Jutel and he slid into the slot of friend. He was ten years younger than her, which wasn't a big deal, but he was so fresh faced and free of baggage. He may be built like a warrior god and the fact that he was Andovian all but assured he was great in bed, but none of that had mattered. Her blushing had been an instinctive response based on embarrassment. She was embarrassed by the fact that he was on the cusp of the prime of his life and she wasn't. He was young and unscarred and she wasn't.

Ultimately that shouldn't matter, and biologically she should probably still be even a little attracted to him. He was gorgeous *and* smart, the only reason she wouldn't be is if her feelings were for someone else. Nians could be screwed up like that. They may have five men to every woman and a small percentage of women really enjoyed that, but the reason their population still hadn't recovered, the reason why most women chose scientific means to conceive their children, was because for thousands of years their people had been monogamous, their bodies had evolved to need that one special connection. When they found it their life spans lengthened and they were, over all, much healthier and happier.

Fighting back a groan Jutel finally admitted to herself that she had feelings for Kisho. She refused to call it love, but what she was feeling was short circuiting her brain and refused to let her look at anyone else in a sexual sense. Thank goodness it wasn't permanent like an Andovian mating ritual. Given time her emotions should lessen to the point where she could move past it. At least that's what she hoped.

Raiden was staring at her. She tried to smile as though she hadn't just had a blindsiding realization, but she ended up making more of a grimace. Her voice cracked when she said, "I was thinking about heading to the center of the city to see the tree and the two rivers thing, uh, the Vende center of life I think it's called, or something like that. You're welcome to tagalong if you want."

His head cocked to the side, his eyes took on an arctic blue tint, and Jutel was reminded that Raiden wasn't just a man but he was part wolf too. The moment passed and whatever his wolf had wanted to check he didn't tell Jutel, instead he said, "Sure that sounds good. First, though, I'd like to make a stop at a Tiger Inc, if that's alright."

"Sure, yeah, that's totally fine."

This time no blush but Jutel wanted to kick herself. She sounded like an idiot, which she wasn't. Damnit she was a Nian warrior that had been tested in both physical and mental battles. She couldn't let a man get her tangled up, especially since she was never going to see him again.

That was a sobering thought. Kisho had made it

clear that he was happy to be leaving them. She'd only had sex with him twice and spent most of her time pissed off at him, of course he didn't want to come back to The Flower and her.

Feeling dejected Jutel tugged on her ear turning off her bio-implants. She wanted more than anything to be alone with her feelings, instead she and Raiden continued toward the center of the city, where she hoped that she'd gain some kind of spiritual insight into the meaning of the universe and something to guide her in her decisions. At the very least, maybe they could find some good food.

Chapter Twenty-Two

Kisho

Sweat dripped from Kisho's hair as pain pulsed through his body. His throat was ravaged by his screams and his voice croaked as he pleaded with his captors to let him go.

"I'm your Imperial Prince, you're committing treason, stop this immediately!"

The two men torturing him exchanged amused smirks before prodding him again with an electrified staff called a boom stick. They'd been at it for an hour with no end in sight. They weren't even asking him any questions. Every now and then they'd whisper to each other, look at him and sneer, then start prodding him again.

He hadn't been given an opportunity to offer up the bio-reader he'd stolen, not that he was at that point—yet. Still they could do something other than torture him. A searing hot heat spread through his body as they jabbed him again with the boom stick. His scream was a guttural primitive noise that did nothing to hide the pain he was feeling.

The room he was in was small, with only a large iron door breaking up the gray walls. There were cameras in every corner, recording everything and projecting it back to whoever wanted to watch. He had no hope that anyone would hear his yells or see the video and rush to his aid, things like that didn't happen on Vende. Of course, things like this weren't supposed to happen either.

His arms were leaden at his side, he'd been unable to fight back before his captors had injected him with something that set his nerves on fire and kept his limbs from moving. He was going nowhere and they knew it.

Almost ready to give up and all but willing his body to die Kisho heard the door behind him clang open. The two psychotic bastards that had been about to start a new round of poke the helpless prince on the floor in a puddle of his own sick snapped to attention. Kisho tried to roll over and see who had come in but he wasn't able to. It ended up not being necessary because as soon as the new comer spoke he knew who it was.

"Cousin, I never expected to see you again."

Fighting back a wave of nausea Kisho's reply was slow and laced with pain. "Taiki, it's been a while. How are you enjoying my throne? I hope it's not too big for you."

There was a pause and Kisho could easily imagine the look of loathing that Taiki had on his face. It was the look he always had when addressing Kisho, as though he were talking to a bug he were about to squash. Only, this was the first time Kisho had ever been at the disadvantage.

A low chuckle filled the air and the two tortures

joined in as back up like the henchmen they were.

"You always thought you were so much better than I was, all because you were going to be emperor and I wasn't. Well look at you now, things didn't turn out how you expected them did they Kisho?"

"Please just kill me now if you're going to tell me how you felt slighted growing up. I have no desire to listen to you complain about your poor pathetic life. Do you even know how I've been living? What it's been like for *me* since I left the palace? Has anyone tried to kill you? Have you been living on the streets?"

Another low chuckle sounded and Kisho stopped talking.

"Who do you think hired the original assassins? You may have been able to avoid death, but I'm the one that decided to be magnanimous in victory. I had the throne, you had a sizable fortune, so I decided to let you live. But here you are, so I'll ask why? Are you trying to regain the throne?"

Shocked Kisho couldn't answer. Not once in all of his wild imaginings did he think his cousin would do something like this. He'd never shown interest in the crown, had always just been a condescending buzzkill. Sure Kisho hated his cousin for having all his money, but he'd never *hated* him.

A hard kick to his stomach brought Kisho out of his stupor. Taiki grabbed Kisho's stringy hair and screamed in his ear, "What are you doing here?"

Grimacing against the assault on his body Kisho said, "I want money. I have undeniable truth that I'm the real heir to the Vende throne and if you want to keep it I demand compensation."

There it was, he'd finally been given the chance to make his proposal. Money for the throne. Hey, it wasn't pretty, but no one actually thought he'd make a good ruler.

The gleam in his cousin's eyes reminded him he needed to add, "Also, if I die the information gets forwarded to all the major news outlets on Vende, then the galaxy. So I don't recommend killing me, because I know there are several people that would love to have a reason to get rid of you."

Well that was a nice look, Taiki's face twisted into a mask of rage. His fists clenched before he started pummeling Kisho. Every cell in Kisho's body was already in pain, but now he was bleeding. Things were not looking up.

Thankfully for him Taiki was not in very good shape and within minutes he'd become winded and unable to continue. Breathing heavily Taiki straightened, taking a towel that was offered to him by one of his henchmen, he started cleaning the blood from his hands.

"I never pegged you as the planning type cousin, not that you've created a very well thought out plan, but once again I'm feeling magnanimous. After all, I hold all the cards. If you think your little fail safe can stop me you're as stupid as I've always thought. I'll offer you a choice."

What choice could Taiki offer Kisho, other than money for the throne? Was he seriously going to consider offering him his life for the bio-reader? If Kisho didn't get money was his life even worth living?

Taiki nodded to his henchmen then turned and left the room. The men grabbed Kisho under his arms and dragged him out of the room. They didn't go far, just into the next chamber where a security system was set up. On one of the several screens was the room they'd been torturing Kisho in, it took a moment for Kisho to understand what was on the other screens though.

When he did a chill went down his spine and suddenly he understood how far his cousin would go to keep the crown. One screen showed Jutel and Raiden standing in line to view the Tree of Life. Raiden seemed bored and he was looking at a group of Venedian women. Jutel was frowning but it didn't appear as though she was looking at anything in particular. Bill and Mal were on another screen sitting at a bar. Mal was talking and Bill was staring into a glass of brown liquid. Dido and Natsuki didn't appear to be on any of the screens and Kisho hoped that they'd managed to escape his cousin's wrath.

His eyes went to his cousins to see how he was going to play this and what he saw there made the bottom fall out of his stomach. "Cousin, these people have done nothing to you—they mean nothing to me, why would you think that I would care what happened to them?"

Taiki smirked at him and Kisho knew he'd screwed up. He cursed himself for being so stupid.

"What do you want?"

"I told you, I'm going to give you a choice and not the choice you think. I'm not going to be so cliché and make you choose between their lives or yours, we both know which you'd choose. No, I want to see if you've grown as a person, I want to know where your priorities are, and just to make sure it doesn't affect your decision I'll promise that whatever you choose you will live and no more harm will come to you."

Frustrated Kisho said, "Get to the point Taiki."

Smirking Taiki inclined his head slightly before

saying, "Either way, you're going to give me the bio-reader, so that's not on the table. What you'll be choosing today is your new friends or the fortune you're seeking."

Incredulous Kisho asked, "Fortune or friends? Really? You're making me choose whether or not I want money or friends? That's easy, money."

His smile widening Taiki chuckled, shaking his head. "You misunderstand cousin, the choice is your friends *lives* or money."

If the two henchmen hadn't been holding Kisho he would have collapsed. Choose between all he'd been working toward or the lives of people he'd only known for a short time? It should be easy, he wasn't known for being anything but selfish. His eyes went to the screen showing Mal and Bill. Did he care about them enough to give everything up? Mal with his odd taste in entertainment and Bill and his just plain oddness?

Easy. Money won in that match. It wasn't just them, though. Jutel changed everything. He watched as she and Raiden inched their way closer to the Tree of Life. The camera, as if sensing his gaze, zoomed in on her face. She looked—sad. Did she miss him? Probably not. He'd been annoying and far from his best.

His head hung low as he remembered every interaction he'd had with her. The fact that she hadn't dumped him at any port they'd passed was a miracle. He'd been bratty and ungracious. Jutel had given him a room and food and not asked for anything and in return he'd hounded her for sex and seriously considered stealing her ship.

Did that change everything? Did that mean that he owed her?

No.

What changed everything were his feelings for her. Maybe if he'd had the opportunity to hook up with another woman and wash her from his system things would have been different, but they weren't. He loved her. She was everything he wasn't. She was strong and kind and didn't deserve to die just because he wanted money. Had things really been so bad without it?

Yes, but if he were the reason that Jutel was killed would he be able to live with himself? Briefly he tried to imagine life where he had money but Jutel was dead and it was surprisingly difficult. Unknown to him she'd creeped into all of his fantasies, even the ones where he was wealthy and throwing around credits like he used too. There were places he wanted to take her, things he wanted to do with her. Not just things that involved sex, but things that involved clothes on, hands off. When had this happened? More importantly, why?

Closing his eyes, unable to continue to look at the monitors, he tried to come up with a way where he could have it all, fortune and Jutel, but Taiki was right, he held all the cards. All of Kisho's careful planning had been a waste.

He tried to comfort himself with the knowledge that there were other ways to make a fortune. At the very least he probably still had a place on The Flower. Given enough time, maybe he could prove to Jutel that he was a changed man and completely worth her time. He'd do everything right this time, he'd woo her, show her that he thought she was a delicate blossom worth taking care of.

"You can keep your money. I'll give you the bio-reader." His words were less forceful than he'd planned but the intent was clear and Taiki looked genuinely shocked, as though it were the last thing he'd expected to hear.

Taking a step toward Kisho, Taiki grabbed his chin and jerked it up so their eyes met. "Are you sure? You're going to choose these relative strangers over a fortune so vast even you can't spend it in a lifetime?"

"Yes." He was even able to keep the regret from his voice when he said it this time.

Taiki stared into his eyes as though searching Kisho's soul. Dropping his chin Taiki took a step back. "I'm genuinely shocked. Never did I think the Imperial Prince Kisho would value people over money. This is going to take me time to process."

Turning to study the monitors Taiko said, "Take them out."

"What? Cousin you said—" Kisho's words were cut off as his vision began to fade and he lost consciences.

Chapter Twenty-Three

Jutel

Jutel woke up groggy with a pounding headache at the base of her skull. Groaning she tried to remember what had she done the night before to get in this shape?

Barely managing to stand she stumbled to her stash of blockers, grabbed the last one there. Within seconds she was feeling relief. Closing her eyes she took a couple deep breaths until the blocker had completely relieved her of the pain. When she opened her eyes she looked at the empty container in front of her and tried to remember when she'd used up her supply. Normally it lasted at least a month. An unfortunate side effect of her bio-implants were frequent headaches so she made sure to have them on hand.

Shaking her head, but unable to come up with an explanation, Jutel tried to recall what she'd done last night to cause such a horrible hangover. The last thing she remembered was being approached by an alien in a bar. He'd threatened to rape her and steal her ship, but she'd handled him. Then what?

Desperately trying to remember, all she kept

drawing was a blank, and her headache returned in full force.

Groaning she lay back down on her bed and curled in around herself. She stayed like that for an hour before she was able to manage the pain. Slowly getting back up, she used the sonic shower to soothe out the last remnants of the pain and then got dressed. The Flower needed to find work and resupply or they weren't going to make it a month and she wasn't ready to go back to Nian yet.

Opening the door she was met with loud yells. She could tell two of the voices were Mal and Bill, but there was a voice she'd never heard before.

"What the hell is going on? I just got rid of my headache, so help me if you give me another one I'm going to be pissed off."

Marching into the fray Jutel separated her friends from the stranger that was somehow on their ship. Pushing him up against the wall, her arm at his throat, she noticed too late that he was an Andovian and that his eyes were glowing. She was now in a narrow hallway with an unknown threat that could potentially rip her to shreds with claws that could sprout out of his hands at any second. Things had gotten complicated fast.

"Who are you? Why are you on my ship?" Her voice was level and she tried to keep her fear under control so the scent of it couldn't set him off.

"I have no idea why I'm on your ship. The last thing I remember I was at home, in my parent's house, on Andove."

Her mind whirled as she tried to explain his presence and the disappearance of her blockers. Something was seriously wrong and it was escalating quickly. Dropping her arm from his neck she took a step back and raised her arms as a show of peace.

"My name is Jutel, you're on my ship The Flower. I have no idea how you got here, but some things aren't making sense for me either. What we need to do now is figure out what happened, to all of us. So just stay calm, no one is going to hurt you."

Her eyes darted to Mal and Bill and judging by their faces they'd found some inconsistencies as well. She took another step back from the Andovian, hoping that it would give him the space he needed. He took several deep breaths and she studied him. He was young, barely a man, but like most Andovians she had met he was broad chested and muscular. He was attractive and it had been a while since Jutel had shared her bed, if the situation were different she'd probably be attracted to him.

"My name is Raiden, my father owns a salvage company, I'm sure if you contacted him he could send men to pick me up. Do you know where we are?"

Her eyes narrowed and she asked, "Is your father Zeke, a wolf-shifter?"

Raiden's eyes grew wide as he nodded. "How did you know? Do you know him?"

"I do. I'm Nian, your parents have dealt with my people before. I had been planning on contacting Zeke for any work he might have, hopefully he'll have some answers to what happened to us. Follow me, we'll go to the cockpit and contact your father. We're only about a week out from Andove so we'll have no problem reaching them."

She started to head straight up, but something on Bill's face stopped her. Going to her friends she grabbed a hand from each and asked, "Are you two okay?"

Mal gave her a small smile and his head titled back as he tried to portray someone that was in control, but behind his eyes she could see that he was worried. Bill didn't even try to hide what he was feeling.

His words were whispered as he tried to keep what he was saying from Raiden, and she didn't bother to tell him that as an Andovian Raiden's hearing would pick up everything said.

"Jutel I can't see the future. Nothing. It's all a fog. I've never felt this before, I was excited at first, but I'm worried. What was done to us? All I remember was looking around that little settlement and then heading back to the ship to join up with you and Mal, then— nothing."

Mal dipped his head down between them and said, "My DVR is cleared of over six weeks of my stories. I'd just connected with the Nian-Earth relay to get the newest episodes and now they've all been deleted, thankfully they're all still recoverable, but the deletion dates looked weird, so I checked the ships log and it's been over six weeks since I linked."

Jutel looked at him blankly as she tried to figure out what he'd said. She nodded her head slowly, her eyes darting to Bill who was rolling his eyes and trying to hide a smile. The important part of what Mal said was pretty big, though.

"So we're missing six weeks?"

"Over six weeks, but yeah."

"That, at least, explains some things. But where did those weeks go? Hopefully Zeke will have some answers."

It took effort not to run to the cockpit after that revelation, but if she lost her cool so would the others.

She had a feeling that right now her calm was the only thing keeping them together.

It was a tight fit but none of them wanted to be left behind and they all needed to know what the hell was going on. However, instead of immediately contacting Zeke, Jutel had to address the flashing communication. Reading the message that popped up Jutel received another clue as to what was going on, though, she still didn't have an answer.

"Apparently we're nowhere near our last location *or* Andove. We're in the space over Vende. We've got docking clearance to land."

"Are we going to Vende or coming from Vende?" Raiden voiced the question they all wanted to know.

Clearing her throat Jutel opened the comms to communicate to the Vende space controller. "Vende Controller this is the Nian ship The Flower."

"Nian ship The Flower, this is Vende Control you need to dock at the provided space or leave the landing queue."

"Affirmative Vende Control. Can you confirm if The Flower has been on Vende before?" Jutel held her breath, it was an odd question and if Vende Control refused to answer she wouldn't be surprised. This comm channel was only for official communication and what she was asking was hardly orthodox. The silence dragged and Jutel started to worry that she'd broken a law or something worse. Vende was known for its order and process when it came to space traffic, it was the only way they were able to process the amount they received.

"Nian ship The Flower, our records do not show a trip to this planet. Please dock or leave the queue."

"Thank you Vende Control, we'll be leaving the queue."

There was no further communication from Vende Control but their docking permission was revoked.

"Now what? Can you communicate with my dad this far out?"

"No, but—" She hesitated before continuing, she didn't know Raiden and what she was about to say wasn't something Nian shared with outsiders. Their communications relay was considered top secret, but right now she had more pressing concerns.

Rubbing her head at the base of her skull where her headache was returning she said, "If we travel a couple days we'll reach a Nian relay and we'll be able to talk there."

"Really? That's crazy, are you sure? I don't know of any relay capable of sending communications that far."

Putting in the coordinates Jutel let Mal answer Raiden's question. She needed to know what was going on. They'd lost over six weeks and while so far the only major change was an added crew member, she doubted that was the cause of their loss in time. Something was missing, something huge, and right now the only clue they had was Raiden. Hopefully Zeke could give them some answers, if not, she didn't know what their next step would be.

As they jumped into hyper speed, she felt a pain in her chest, like she was leaving something important behind. Watching the stars streak outside the window she tried desperately to remember what it was but the pounding against her skull just became more insistent.

Rubbing her eyes she hoped that she'd made the right decision.

Epilogue

Kisho

Kisho watched the screen as The Flower left Vende space. When Jutel's voice came over the comms he'd hoped that she'd say she was coming for him, that she knew what had been done, and nothing would stop her. Instead she'd left.

Taiki grinned at him before leaving the room. His henchmen grabbed Kisho under his arms and dragged him from the bowels of the civic building he'd been in this entire time. Taking him out back, they dumped him in a dark, dank alley.

He lay there for hours as the paralytic they'd given him worked its way out of his system. He was alone, again, only this time he didn't have a driving force guiding him. The bio-reader was gone, all the backups surely destroyed, and he had no hope of ever regaining his fortune. What hurt the most, though, was that his friends and the woman he loved had no idea who he was or that he even existed.

Where did he go from here?

Author's Note

Thanks for reading "Guiding Light", I fell in love with Jutel while writing "Deception" and I couldn't resist writing her story. I'm currently working on the sequel to "Guiding Light" and I'll have it out as quickly as I can since I know how frustrating a cliffhanger can be.

For those that have been asking, I have plans to continue my Nians on Earth series and while writing "Guiding Light" I got an idea for my Twin Moons of Andove series. Lots of books in the works!

I love this universe and I hope you do too.

If you enjoyed this story, one of the best things you can do is leave a review *and* if you would like to be notified of future installments in the series please sign up for my mailing list.

Cassandralogan.com

About the Author

Cassandra Logan lives in central North Carolina with her husband, daughter, and their two cats. When she's not writing she spends her time reading, binge-watching Netflix, and baking sinfully delicious deserts.

She is the author of the Nians on Earth series and the Twin Moons of Andove series. She is currently working on expanding that universe.

Cassandralogan.com

Character List

Anika- Andovian wolf-shifter, artist, married to Zeke, mother to Raiden.

Bill- Olovian psychic, freed by a Nian diplomatic party, joins Jutel and Mal for excitement

Captain Fah- United Universe Aid Coalition captain station near Andove

Dido- Venedian that is picked up on the planet Benjo

Jutel- Nian warrior, after a series of setbacks she's doubting herself and searching the universe for answers

Kisho- Imperial Prince of Vende, thief, trying to regain his fortune

Malikina 'Mal'- Nian cultural expert, loves Earth Soap Operas, best friends with Jutel and seeking to find his place in the universe

Natsuki- Infant girl that is picked up on Benjo with Dido

Pinzan- Andovian and owner of a salvage company that rivals Zeke's

Raiden- Andovian, Anika and Zeke's oldest son, wolf-shifter, looking for adventure, very good with tech

Taiki- His Majesty the Emperor of Vende, cousin to Kisho

Talina- Nian ambassador and leader of Jutel and Mal's first mission

Zeke- Andovian wolf-shifter, owner of a salvage company, married to Anika, father to Raiden

Series Information

The Fringes of the Universe
Book One: "Guiding Light"
Book Two: COMING SOON!

Twin Moons of Andove Series
Book One: "Abducted"
Book Two: "Stolen"
Book Three: "Hunted"
Book Four: "Deception"

Nians on Earth Series
Book Zero: "Nians on Earth Prequel"
Book One: "Destiny"
Book Two: "Desire"
Book Three: "Delight"
Book Four: "Deception"

Standalone Stories
"Santa's Scrooge: A Christmas Short Story"
"Witches of Cadence Cove Shorts Vol. 1"